Praise for *Kai'Ro*

personally excited about the work Judah
of influence in the urban context fleshed
honored to support him."
—**LECRAE**, Hip Hop recording artist

The story of Kai'Ro shows the effects of how one man's choice to relocate
to his old neighborhood with the hope of the gospel makes a profound
impact on changing his city for Christ."
—**JOHN PERKINS**, founder of Christian Community Development
    Association

"I tried to find something that my guys could relate to and identify with,
and at the same time help to teach the Bible. I thought, let me try *Kai'Ro*
with the boys. Imagine about 17 young guys listening to me read the book
. . . the guys ate it up! They loved it so much that, at the end of each
chapter, they wanted me to keep reading."
—**ALONZO BROWN JR.**, Common Ground Ministry, Montgomery, Alabama

"I wanna be like Kai'Ro because he cares about what God, his only King,
thinks about him."
—**JAQUARIUS**, 13 years old

"My favorite character in the book is Kai'Ro because he wants to change
his life around, even though his friends didn't want to change their lives;
it made me want to be like Kai'Ro."
—**RONDALE**, 12 years old

"This book gives hope for those who messed up. God takes the burden of
our sins and changes our lives."
—**KENDAL**, 17 years old

"KAI★RO"

THE JOURNEY OF AN URBAN PILGRIM

by JUDAH BEN

MOODY PUBLISHERS
CHICAGO

© 2013
JUDAH BEN

Scriptures are based on the author's paraphrase of the Holy Bible, English Standard Version.

Edited by Kathryn Hall
Interior Designer: Design Corps
Cover Design and Image: Geoffrey Sciacca

Library of Congress Cataloging-in-Publication Data

Ben, Judah.
  Kai'Ro : the journey of an urban pilgrim / Judah Ben.
    pages cm
  ISBN 978-0-8024-0664-4
  1. Bunyan, John, 1628-1688. Pilgrim's progress—Adaptations. 2. Christian fiction. I. Title.
PS3602.E6557K35 2013
813'.6—dc23

                                                                2012048540

We hope you enjoy this book from Moody Publishers. Our goal is to provide high-quality, thought-provoking books and products that connect truth to your real needs and challenges. For more information on other books and products written and produced from a biblical perspective, go to www.moodypublishers.com or write to:

Moody Publishers
820 N. LaSalle Boulevard
Chicago, IL 60610

1 3 5 7 9 10 8 6 4 2

Printed in the United States of America

To my students at Restoration Academy.
May you find and keep to the little dirt road
that lies just beyond the hedges.

CONTENTS

DREAMIN'

STORYTELLER: Some folks would say it was a dream. They may be right, but what I witnessed that night truly changed my life.

I saw before me a terrible looking prison situated under a dark night sky. The tall brick walls were topped with twisted coils of razor wire. From the watchtowers, a red and sinister glow eerily radiated. An old sign stood out front and, in chipped paint, it read END OF THE ROAD JAIL: A HOME FOR THE HOPELESS.

My dream suddenly took me inside, where I walked through the shadowy halls until I was taken into a room lined with cells. Within those small spaces were men and women, young and old, caged like filthy animals. Some of them were chained to walls like leashed dogs. They could hardly move. Others were curled up in the corners of their chambers, shivering from the cold and from fear. Many of them were nearly naked. Several were bloody and bruised, as if they had been tortured or thrashed by some merciless being.

I heard loud groans and deafening cries. I saw people pressed up against the bars with tears streaming down their faces. There were others bound up like crazy people. They rolled around on the floor or beat their heads against the wall, cursing and shouting.

Then I saw a young man who looked like he could be no older than eighteen. Sitting on the ground of his cell, he was dressed in baggy jeans and wearing a dirty wife beater. I noticed there were some bad bruises on his face and that his knuckles were cracked and covered with dried blood. By the small shaft of moonlight coming through his cell window, he was writing a letter. It read:

Evangeline,

This may be the last letter I write you for a while, girl. Preacher stopped in to see me again today and this time I made my decision. Like I said to you this morning when you came by, I think our whole town is about to come to a terrible end. I think all of us are in trouble. The City of Doom is going to be judged.

You know, Preacher broke some things down for me. He told me that if I was willing to get out of town and head out onto the Heavenly Highway, there'd be hope for me, for real. I still can't believe you laughed when I told you that. Don't you feel it, girl? Don't you feel that terrible burden on your back? I sure do feel mine! It's a burden of guilt, regret, pain and shame. I started feeling it a long time ago, but I guess I did a good job of ignoring it.

Preacher also told me that my burden was my soul crying out to be free. He's right. I want to be free, for real. And I don't just mean from this lousy jail cell. I want true freedom. Preacher said the King has the freedom I need and want. And so, by the time you find this letter, I'll be gone. My homies, Quitter and Follower, are getting out of here tomorrow too. They said they want to go with me.

I wish to God that you'd think this thing over and come with me. I'm telling you, Evangeline, this City of Doom we've been living in is going to get burned up. You need to get out while you still can. Come to your senses, girl! I pray you do. If you come looking for me, just follow the dirt road that's past the hedge of bushes at the edge of town. It's a real trail because I've been there once before. Don't waste no more time. You need to come now!

I'll always love you.

Your boy,

Kai'Ro

THE DIRT ROAD

STORYTELLER: Kai'Ro put the letter in an envelope, got up from the floor and walked over to his cot. Sitting on the edge of the shabby, makeshift bed, he picked up a black Bible and started reading it. His lips moved slightly as he read the words. Every now and then, he'd stop and stare off. Sometimes he'd smile like someone who had just learned some great news. He read and read through the dark of night until the sun started to fill the window of his cell with bright light.

As my dream suddenly shifted, I saw Kai'Ro and two other young men about his age standing by the curb just outside the jail. All three of them were squinting in the noonday sun.

KAI'RO: So, ya'll ready to do this, for real?

FOLLOWER: Yeah, man, you know that I'll go wit you wherever you go. I mean, we grew up together in this town, dawg. You think I'm 'bout to just let you roll on outta here by yourself? Naw, I'm goin' wit you.

QUITTER: I mean, I ain't lettin' ya'll just leave me here. I don't understand what all the hype's about, but I'm down.

KAI'RO: Cool. Well, let's go home and get cleaned up. We can pack our things and meet by the hedges on the edge of town.

QUITTER: You mean the ones right off of EXCUSES STREET, right?

KAI'RO: Yeah, those are the ones. Did ya'll write your letters?

STORYTELLER: Quitter and Follower looked at each other and then back at Kai'Ro. Follower cleared his throat.

FOLLOWER: I meant to do it, man, but I fell asleep last night, dawg. My bad. I'll write my girl when we get on the road.

KAI'RO: How 'bout you, Quitter? You write yours?

QUITTER: Naw, homie. I told ya my girl would snap on me if I sent her that kinda letter and then went slinkin' out of the house on her. You craaazy? I'm just gonna bounce on outta town wit ya'll, and that's that. She'll prob'ly just figure I'm off doin' one of my things.

KAI'RO: You shoulda written your letters. Both of you. I told ya'll, I ain't comin' back here once I'm gone. I love Evangeline as much as you love your girls. But she wasn't down with this whole trip, for real. I told her 'bout it every time she came to visit me. She kept laughin' and tellin' me I was just messed up from bein' locked up. I warned her that I'd do this thing alone. That's why I wrote that letter. She's goin' to have to come after me, 'cause I'm bouncin'.

FOLLOWER: Look, let's just get goin'. I don't wanna waste no more time arguin'.

STORYTELLER: The three young men split up and hurried to their homes. When Kai'Ro got to his place, he quickly went through the drawers of his dresser. Pulling a backpack from under his bed, he stuffed it with fresh clothes and a small wad of cash that he'd kept hidden. Finally, he removed a black gun from his bottom drawer and shoved it in the bag.

After a quick shower, Kai'Ro threw on a pair of clean baggy jeans, a black tall-T, some shiny Js and a NY cap. He took the letter that he had written in the jail the night before, kissed it, placed it on Evangeline's pillow and then disappeared out the front door.

The air was stifling under the intense heat. After he walked for a while down the sidewalk, a few thuggish looking guys on a porch nodded and waved. One of them hollered to him as he passed by.

PAIN: What up, Kai'Ro? So you finally free, dawg?

KAI'RO: Man, I wish.

PAIN: What'cha mean? You outta the joint, ain't you?

KAI'RO: No doubt, but my soul ain't free yet. Gotta get my soul freed up.

PAIN: For real? What'cha mean by that? You goin' to go to church or somethin'?

KAI'RO: I can't really explain it yet, dawg. That's why I'm bouncin' up outta here. I'm headin' out to the Heavenly Highway.

PAIN: The Heavenly who?

KAI'RO: Heavenly Highway, homie. It's gonna lead me to the Cross, and it's gonna lead me to freedom from the burden I got. You know the row of bushes over there where EXCUSES STREET and BONDAGE BOULEVARD meet?

PAIN: Yeah. What about it?

KAI'RO: Head through the bushes sometime, playa. You'll find the trail...

STORYTELLER: Kai'Ro smiled at Pain and then waved him good-bye. Pain and his gang watched him disappear out of sight. After a few more blocks, Kai'Ro came to the wall of bushes that he had described. Quitter and Follower showed up just like they promised.

QUITTER: This is craaazy, dawg. I can't believe we're actually doin' this.

FOLLOWER: Man, people 'round here are goin' to flip when they hear what we're doin'.

KAI'RO: Preacher said to move quickly. He said there wasn't much time left. He told me to head out of the City to the Crossroads and then on to the Gate. He said that once I got to the Crossroads I'd have to make a decision to either take the Heavenly Highway or the Path of Least Resistance.

QUITTER: So, what's up with the Crossroads? I mean, why can't Preacher dude just tell us which way to go? I don't get it.

KAI'RO: Preacher said that the Heavenly Highway leads all the way to the City of Light. But every man has to choose for himself.

QUITTER: So, is there somethin' wrong with the Path of Least Resistance?

KAI'RO: Preacher said that the Path of Least Resistance is the easier road to take.

QUITTER: Man, then why would we wanna make things any harder on ourselves?

KAI'RO: Because the man said that the Path of Least Resistance is wide, flat and smooth at first. But the further down that road you go, you eventually work your way into the Alley of Few Opportunities. According to Preacher, the Alley is wide at first; but the further you go, the tighter it gets. It's gradual, he said, but as you walk down the Path, the walls of the Alley get closer and closer to the road. And after a while, the way gets so tight that you actually get stuck and can't go nowhere but backwards. He also told me to watch carefully 'cause there are plenty of holes along the way and that a lot of travelers never even make it very far.

FOLLOWER: I'm with Quitter. I don't see how a road with a name like that can be so bad. I bet Preacher never even went down that road. Some of them Holy Roller guys think it's cool to do things the hard way just so they can feel good about themselves. Know what I'm sayin'? It's like goin' uphill is somehow a strategy to get somewhere and to be somebody. Man, I've always found it easier to just chill. I'd rather use my brain to find the easiest way to get somethin' done. Why waste my time climbin' and clawin' when I can be chillin'?

QUITTER: That's for real, dawg.

KAI'RO: I'm just tellin' you what Preacher told me. I believe him. I think he was shootin' straight with me.

STORYTELLER: After taking a deep breath, Kai'Ro led the way and pushed ahead into the bushes. The other two stopped for a moment, looked at each other, and then followed after him. The bushes were thick and thorny, snagging and pulling at their T-shirts and jeans. Both Quitter and Follower complained as the branches scratched their skin and tore holes in their shirts.

QUITTER: Ah c'mon, dawg! This shirt cost me like thirty dollars!

STORYTELLER: Kai'Ro kept going and pushed the branches aside with his hands until they came out on the other side. As he had promised them a few days earlier, there was a small dirt trail that headed off into the countryside. The path was almost invisible with a lot of weeds growing on it. Kai'Ro wiped away some sweat from his forehead and waved at his friends to come on. After a while, the three men walked out into the green, open countryside.

KAI'RO: It's nice out here, isn't it?

QUITTER: You been out here before?

KAI'RO: Once. I heard about it, so I felt like I had to check it out. I didn't go real far, though. I hadn't planned to stay so I turned back. But, it's nice and quiet.

FOLLOWER: Yeah, it smells nice out here too. There's no pollution, graffiti, trash or nothin'.

KAI'RO: (with a faraway look in his eyes) The last time I was out here, I had only walked a little ways, and then I just sat down on that stone over there. Man, I sat there for like an hour and just did nothin'. It was so peaceful. I can't explain it, but I just didn't wanna leave...all the plants and the wind in the trees...I guess I never really knew how nice it could be, until I got out here and actually experienced it. It was just good to get away from all that drama in the city.

QUITTER: Man, if it's like this all the way, you can count me in, dawg. This *is* nice out here.

STORYTELLER: The three friends walked for a long time and passed some beautiful places; including a deep blue lake, some giant rocks and some lush green woods. They continued to follow the dirt path, which was just wide enough for the three of them to walk shoulder to shoulder. At times, they walked quietly. Sometimes, they pointed at all the amazing sights around them.

After a while, the young men spotted a large building perched on a hill with a tall Vegas-looking sign that read "The House of Mockers." Though they were still a ways off, the travelers could feel the pounding of music and bass hitting them like eighteen-inch woofers in a '64 Impala on switches. They could also hear the laughter of women.

Looking at each other in total surprise, they tried to figure out what the strange place was all about. So they moved closer until the building was slightly elevated just above them. It was made of grey bricks and all of the windows were tinted. But from the outside, they could see bright lights flashing behind the glass. In the parking lot in front of the House of Mockers, a bunch of young guys and girls were laughing, smoking and carrying on.

FOLLOWER: Yo, what *is* this place? Check out the girls up there.

QUITTER: Man, you ain't playin'. Shoot, homie, I just got the urge to take a 'lil rest. What'cha say, Kai'Ro?

KAI'RO: I think we should keep goin'. Preacher said it would take all day to get to the Crossroads. Then just beyond the Crossroads there'll be a place for us to rest. I wanna get there before dark. Preacher warned that there are some brothas on this road that we wouldn't wanna tangle with after dark. So let's bounce on outta here.

FOLLOWER: Aww, come on, Kai'Ro! We could stop in and grab somethin' to drink. And maybe get one of those female's digits. How's it gonna hurt?

KAI'RO: Listen, Follower, I set out on this journey 'cause the stuff that's goin' on in that place bothers me. It didn't always used to, but it does now. Preacher told me I'd have to give that stuff up...the girls, the clubbin', the 40s—all of it. Trust me, I wanna go in there too. But when I think about it, the burden on my back gets even heavier. I've *got* to get rid of this burden. I've just got to.

STORYTELLER: As Kai'Ro finished speaking, one of the men in the parking lot hollered at them. When he did, all of the others stopped to stare at the three travelers on the path.

PARTYCAT: Yo, is that you, Kai'Ro? Man, I ain't seen you in the longest.

KAI'RO: Hey, P.C. What's up?

PARTYCAT: Nuttin' much. Man, come up here and have a smoke with us.

KAI'RO: Can't, homie. We're on our way somewhere else.

PARTYCAT: Somewhere else? Where? Man, you've found the only place you need to be right here.

KAI'RO: I don't get down like that no more. Not for real.

PARTYCAT: Man, you're trippin'. I've got three honeys here right now that are just itchin' to dance with you and ya boys. It'll be my treat, my way of sayin' welcome to the House of Mockers.

FREAKY: Hey, Kai'Ro. Why don't you come up here and come on inside. I've never disappointed nobody.

STORYTELLER: Freaky stepped out from behind Partycat. She was wearing some tight shorts and an even tighter white, low-cut T-shirt. She pointed at Kai'Ro and tried to draw him into the House with her finger.

PARTYCAT: You hear the music in there? Man, it's bangin'. Quit wastin' your time out there. Get in here and party with us, dawg.

KAI'RO: I appreciate it, man, but we gotta keep goin'. We're off to the Crossroads and then on to the Heavenly Highway.

STORYTELLER: When Kai'Ro told the crew where he and his friends were going, the entire crowd burst into laughter. Some of the girls rolled their eyes and all the guys cracked up, pointing at Kai'Ro, Quitter and Follower. Partycat took a long draw from his cigar and blew the smoke out slowly. Then he glared at Kai'Ro and growled.

PARTYCAT: Now I know you trippin'. Since when did Kai'Ro from the City of Doom say no to some dancin' and havin' a good time with a fine woman?

FREAKY: Yeah, what's your problem, boy? You don't like girls no more?

KAI'RO: Of course, I like girls! You craaazy? I'm just not down with this whole scene no more. I left the City of Doom and I'm off to find Life and the freedom it brings. So get up off me, I'm fixin' to bounce up outta here!

PARTYCAT: Life! Freedom! Man, look around here, playa'. There's no more life and freedom than what you gonna find right here in this building. Man, I've got more life and more freedom waitin' inside than you'll see in a lifetime.

KAI'RO: It's not the same. I want Life and freedom for my soul. I've had all that other stuff and it didn't satisfy me. Not for long anyway. I've been to clubs just like this a hundred times. I've had more girlfriends than I can remember. Man, I've done just about anything a dude can do, and it left me wantin' more every time. It was like eatin' from the same plate every day—but never gettin' enough... always leavin' the table feelin' hungry again. Now I've got an appetite deep inside that's just groanin' away. It's a hunger for somethin' that'll last forever. I guess you don't understand what kinda freedom I'm talkin' about.

PARTYCAT: Freedom for your soul, huh? A hunger for... man, since when did you get all religious on me? Maybe I oughta come down there and slap some sense into your thick head. Maybe you and your friends oughta step out of here before me and my boys make all of y'all hurt.

FOLLOWER: Man, forget this! C'mon, Kai'Ro, let's clown this fool. No one's gonna treat us and get away with it! You goin' to let this fool talk to us like that, dawg?

QUITTER: Man, you know I won't back down!

KAI'RO: (holding Follower back) We're on our way, P.C. No need for any hostility. I'm different now. That's why we're leavin'. We're gone.

PARTYCAT: Yeah, get gone, clown. Step on outta here before I change my mind. You and your lil' weak friends won't find anything down that road but loneliness and disappointment.

STORYTELLER: As the three friends took off down the trail, they were followed by a sea of laughter. Partycat and his crowd hollered insults at them, cursing and mocking them until they were finally out of sight.

QUITTER: Man, if you weren't one of my best friends, I woulda' never gone through all that drama. You didn't do a thing! Man, for real, I was ready to climb up there and knock that cat's head off. He called us weak and dissed us big time. And you just stood there! What's happenin' to you?

FOLLOWER: For real, man. I've never seen you like that before. Boys back in the City of Doom would be lookin' for their teeth right now after sayin' stuff like that to you. But you did nothin' and made us look like a buncha girls.

KAI'RO: Look, every inch of me wanted to go in that House with that girl and get with her. Plus, everything that P.C. called us ticked me off. I was achin' to grab my piece and smoke him right there. No one ever called me those names before and got away with it. *Nobody!*

But it's like I said, I don't feel the same. I've got an urge to get to the Crossroads and to get on that Heavenly Highway. It's the only way I can lose this wretched burden on my back. It's drivin' me insane, and it's more important to be free from my burden than anything. Do ya'll not feel one pressin' in on you right now?

QUITTER: I feel nothin'. I'm just really mad right now.

FOLLOWER: Me too.

STORYTELLER: The House of Mockers experience left the three friends at odds with one another. So the men continued to walk down the path in silence. Kai'Ro led the way as the other two followed behind with their heads hanging low. Quitter and Follower no longer seemed too excited about the trip.

In time, they passed through more open and beautiful spaces. But somehow they had lost interest and paid no attention. Soon they came to a part of the path that disappeared into some tall grass that nearly reached up to their shoulders. Their pace slowed, but Kai'Ro tried hard to keep his eyes on the path. They walked in a single line with Follower close at Kai'Ro's heels and Quitter a few steps behind. Suddenly, Kai'Ro let out a loud cry as he and Follower fell into a thick swamp.

FOLLOWER: (yelling) Man, what in the world! What is this?

KAI'RO: I dunno.

FOLLOWER: What do you mean, you don't know? Man, I didn't come all this way to fall into no swamp. No way!

STORYTELLER: Kai'Ro and Follower thrashed around in the water. But the more they thrashed, the deeper they sank into the mud.

QUITTER: (reaching down and grabbing a loose branch) Man, this is stupid! Look. Grab this stick and I'll pull ya'll outta there. Then let's get back on dry ground and head back home. I can't believe I did this!

FOLLOWER: Yeah. C'mon, Kai'Ro, let's get outta here. This whole trip is a joke, man. I can't believe I let you talk me into this mess!

KAI'RO: I'm not goin' back, ya'll. I can't go back now. Preacher said we'd go through some stuff. I'm goin' on to the other side.

STORYTELLER: Follower turned around and grabbed ahold of the stick that Quitter was holding out to him. Kai'Ro kept thrashing and struggling, but he just sank deeper and deeper. Eventually, Follower got out and started scraping the mud and crud off of his clothes with his hands. He began cursing when he looked at his muddy Js and his dirty, wet jeans. Both he and Quitter hollered at Kai'Ro to turn around and join them.

KAI'RO: Look, ya'll don't understand. I'm not goin' back. I'm goin' on. I gotta go on.

FOLLOWER: Man, now I know what Partycat was sayin' back there. You are a fool. I don't get it, dawg. You're gonna drown out there by yourself. Just turn around and grab ahold of this stick and we'll pull you out.

KAI'RO: Jump in here and join me. It ain't that far to the other side. I can see it from here.

STORYTELLER: By now, both Follower and Quitter were cursing at their friend and shaking their fists at him. But it didn't take them long to figure out that his mind wasn't going to change. They waved their hands at him in disgust and took off back towards where they had come.

When Kai'Ro realized that he was all alone, he tried even harder to get to the other side. But he just kept sinking deeper and deeper. I could see that he was starting to panic. The mud in the swamp was sucking him down. He called out for help and held up his arms. Just then, a man came rushing towards him.

HELPER: Hold on! Don't give up!

STORYTELLER: The man was running along a stone path beside the marsh. He got right up on Kai'Ro and extended him a hand. With a big tug, the man hauled him out of the mud. Kai'Ro fell down on the ground, gasping for air.

HELPER: You'll be all right, brotha. Why didn't you take the stone path?

KAI'RO: (coughing) Man! I didn't see it, for real. I was just walkin' along. Then all of a sudden, I fell in that awful swamp.

HELPER: The Swamp of Discouragement has gotten a lot of brothas early in their trip to the Heavenly Highway. Dudes get stuck, give up and never come back. Did you come alone?

KAI'RO: No. I had two of my best friends with me. But they went back and left me alone.

HELPER: Yeah. So many people lose heart at this terrible Swamp. The King built this stone path alongside it for travelers like you. But the mud often shifts, the grass grows high and the path is hard to find.

KAI'RO: I couldn't see it for nuthin'.

HELPER: Don't get discouraged, dawg. Your eyes are new to this path. As you keep goin' on this journey, your eyes will grow stronger. You'll get used to seein' the blessings and little help-ful things the King has left for you along the way.

STORYTELLER: Kai'Ro stood up and started wiping the mud and slime off of his pants and shirt.

KAI'RO: I just feel stupid. I feel real stupid.

HELPER: The fact that you kept going shows courage, and it shows that you're committed. I'm glad I could lend a hand. The King has kept me here to help out brothas like you when they get stuck.

KAI'RO: Thanks, man.

HELPER: No problem. Now get goin'. There's still time left in the day.

STORYTELLER: Kai'Ro shook Helper's hand and then headed off again. Alone this time, he walked for a while down the dirt path. I could tell that he was thinking hard.

WORLDLY WISEMAN

STORYTELLER: After a while, I could see a man coming towards Kai'Ro from the opposite direction. The man was dressed in a flashy green and black suit. He wore alligator boots, shiny rimmed glasses, and carried a cane. Sporting a big gold chain with a cross on it, he came up to Kai'Ro and started talking to him.

WORLDLY WISEMAN: Yo, what's good, son? The name's Worldly Wiseman.

KAI'RO: W'sup?

WORLDLY WISEMAN: What happened to you? You look like you got it rough, man.

KAI'RO: Yeah, I fell into the Swamp of Discouragement back there. It's all good now.

WORLDLY WISEMAN: The Swamp of Discouragement? Man, where you headin', playa?

KAI'RO: I'm headin' to the Crossroads and then on to the Gate and the Heavenly Highway.

WORLDLY WISEMAN: (laughing) So, my man got some religion, huh? Who put the Heavenly Highway in your head, son?

KAI'RO: Preacher. He's a good man.

WORLDLY WISEMAN: Man, that ol' fool? Son, that man ain't worth the cheap suits he wears to church on Sundays. He got you confused. Let me ask you somethin'. You got a girl?

KAI'RO: Yeah. I got a girl back home, in the City of Doom.

WORLDLY WISEMAN: You just left her back there, man? Why? She did you wrong or somethin'?

KAI'RO: No, it wasn't like that. She was a good girl. I mean, she and I were real tight.

WORLDLY WISEMAN: Son, were you good to her, or did you have a little play goin' on the side?

KAI'RO: Naw, it wasn't like that. We were both real true to each other. I just had to move on. I've got this doggone burden on my back. Until I get free of it, there just ain't no peace for me, for real.

WORLDLY WISEMAN: I 'spose Preacher told you 'bout the burden too.

KAI'RO: Yeah, but . . .

WORLDLY WISEMAN: You left your girl and all your friends 'cause you was listenin' to Preacher? Boy, you must be crazy.

KAI'RO: Yeah? A lot of people have been tellin' me that, but what's drivin' me crazy is this burden. I mean, this burden keeps me up nights. Besides, he wasn't the only one who got me goin' on this road. He was just the final spark.

WORLDLY WISEMAN: What you mean?

STORYTELLER: Kai'Ro reached into his pant pocket and pulled out his old, tattered black Book.

KAI'RO: I been readin' this Bible. This was Granddaddy's. He gave it to Pops, but Pops didn't read it much. He split when I was three and the Book stayed in Mama's bedroom for years. She used to read it to us every now and then, but not much. I started readin' in it a few months ago, and it's been sayin' the same thing as Preacher. It says I got a real problem inside. It says that I offend God with my sin. It even says that my town and everybody that I know is gonna get burned up. Unless I get rid of this burden, I'm goin' down right along with it.

WORLDLY WISEMAN: (laughing) Man, that ol' Preacher and that Book has got you scared, bro. There's a lot of brothas and sistas who come down this way, complainin' about their burden. They go on yappin' about how they're goin' to the Crossroads and on to the Heavenly Highway. Man, I got a way to get rid of that burden, and you ain't gotta go to all that trouble. You ain't gotta go on and waste all your time.

KAI'RO: Whatcha' mean, man?

WORLDLY WISEMAN: (pointing) Do you see that hill over there?

STORYTELLER: Kai'Ro turned to his left and saw a tall, grassy hill. On the top, there were several large houses. He stared at the hill for a while.

KAI'RO: What about that hill?

WORLDLY WISEMAN: I got a friend up there, man. He specializes in removin' those burdens.

KAI'RO: What are you talkin' 'bout?

WORLDLY WISEMAN: His name is Mac-Morality. And that little suburb, man, that's Legalopolis. My boy Mac's been removin' burdens for a real long time. Most of those folks up there were travelers just like you. All of them were complainin' about this *burden* and how they just had to get rid of it. They were on their way to the Heavenly Highway when they met Mac and got things straightened out by him.

STORYTELLER: It was clear to me that Kai'Ro's mind was spinning. He stared at Worldly Wiseman like he didn't know if the man could be trusted. I wondered what decision he would make.

KAI'RO: That sounds good, but what you're sayin' doesn't sound at all like what Preacher said.

WORLDLY WISEMAN: Look, you need to forget about Preacher. He's a looney old man who's filled a lot of people's heads with nothin' but trouble and guilt. Mac is all about givin' people peace and givin' it to 'em fast.

Listen, what you're missin' is balance. You almost had it back in the City of Doom, but you were a little off. Man, it sounds to me like you had it goin' on. You have a good girl. She's good to you and you're good to her. That's all that matters, for real. Keep your nose clean. Stay out of the real deep stuff, you know, the type of stuff that'll get you in serious trouble.

You're almost there already, son. Mac will set you straight. Shoot, who knows? Maybe you and your girl can leave that city of yours and all that drama behind. You'll get a new perspective up there on Legalopolis. Ya'll could move up there.

KAI'RO: Well, I wanna get rid of this burden. It's killin' me. I'll head on up there and talk to ya boy, Mac. If he can set me straight, then I'm game.

STORYTELLER: Worldly Wiseman flashed a big, gold-toothed smile and slapped Kai'Ro on the back.

WORLDLY WISEMAN: Now, that's what I'm talkin' 'bout! When Mac sets you straight, you'll be lookin' me up to say thank you.

KAI'RO: I appreciate it. I'll holler at you.

STORYTELLER: With that, Kai'Ro turned off the dirt trail and headed for the green hill. But when he got there, it was much steeper and scarier than it first appeared. In fact, standing at the bottom and looking up, it almost seemed to bend up and over him. As he studied the hill, he noticed a small trail that zigzagged back and forth along the front of it.

Very cautiously, Kai'Ro put his right foot forward. Discovering that the surface was slick, he braced himself with his hand. Immediately, he cried out as one of the stones cut him. He tried again, but his burden and the awkwardness of the path made the going real hard.

Kai'Ro was only able to get a few feet up the path before he tripped and stumbled and fell back down to the bottom. That made him real mad and caused him to curse the ground. When he looked up, he saw Preacher coming towards him. Embarrassed, he hung his head.

PREACHER: Son, what are you doing here?

KAI'RO: Someone said that I could lose my burden up there. At the time, I thought it sounded like a good idea.

PREACHER: And who told you *that*?

KAI'RO: Worldly Wiseman told me about a man named Mac-Morality who could free me of this burden by helpin' me balance and order my life. It sounded good. It even sounded—

PREACHER: (interrupting him) Did it *really* sound *good* to you, son? I mean, deep down in your soul, did it sound right?

KAI'RO: (sighing) Not for real. I mean, yeah, it sounded good to my ears that I could get free of this burden. But in my soul, it didn't sit right.

PREACHER: Things are changing in you, Kai'Ro. You aren't seeing and hearing things the same way anymore, are you? Your soul wants freedom and that freedom isn't going to come on the top of that hill. Didn't Helper promise you that, as you journey down the road, you'd begin to see things differently?

KAI'RO: Yeah.

PREACHER: You'll have to be careful because there are others more cunning than Worldly Wiseman, who will seek to take you off the path. Some will make pleasant sounding promises that will prove to be nothing but lies. Others will seek to destroy you entirely, my son. Now, let me show you something.

STORYTELLER: Preacher walked a little ways along the edge of the hill over to some tall grass. Kai'Ro followed close by. The wise man then parted some of the grass and showed Kai'Ro a large pile of bricks, a shattered window frame, a busted door, and what looked like a bed mattress, some cabinets, and a kitchen table. Clearly, it was the ruins of an old house.

PREACHER: Do you know where all this stuff came from?

STORYTELLER: Kai'Ro looked at Preacher for a minute and then took a hard look up towards the hill.

PREACHER: Yes, son. That house was once up there. The top of that hill is nothing but brittle rock and sand. Those who do make it up there find the view to be splendid. But when the winds start to blow or a violent storm whips across the terrain, many of those homes tumble down. There are more fallen houses just like this one scattered all around here.

   Mac and his ilk are selling nothing but lies. They can't free you or anyone else from their burden. The good life they offer is only a myth.

KAI'RO: I was wrong to doubt you. I'm sorry.

PREACHER: You were wrong to doubt the Truth. Knowing the Truth is what's going to set you free.

KAI'RO: I'm only a day into this thing. So far, I got harassed by a bunch of guys and girls back down the way. My two homeboys left me high and dry. Then I fell and almost sank in the Swamp of Discouragement. I'm tired already. This walk is a beast, for real.

PREACHER: It is a beast. Yet, when you get to the foot of the Cross and your burden rolls away, you will know and taste life as never before. I can't put it any plainer than that. The tug in your heart is genuine. It's a tug for Life. *Abundant* Life. Listen, only the Cross can free your burden, for real. Remember, nothing else will work. Nothing.

KAI'RO: Well, I'd best be goin' then. Maybe I can make it to the Crossroads before it gets dark.

PREACHER: You're almost there. Goodwill at the Gate will take you in for the night. Peace be unto you, my son.

STORYTELLER: Kai'Ro said goodbye and then hurried along on the dirt trail again. Moving quickly because he knew that he had to make up some lost time, he walked along for quite a while. Sometimes he'd hum, and other times he'd throw on his headphones and bob his head to one of the gospel tracks he'd made in the studio.

After some time passed, he crossed over a small hill and then came to a sudden fork in the road. An old, beat-up sign pointed to a wide and well-traveled road to the left. The words on the sign read PATH OF LEAST RESISTANCE. This road appeared smooth, paved, and level as far as the eye could see.

To the right was a narrow road just wide enough for a man and his friend. The sign for this road read HEAVENLY HIGHWAY. The path was bumpy, full of twists and turns, and it was so steep that Kai'Ro groaned at the sight of it. Although similar to the path on the hill leading up to Legalopolis, it appeared to me much less traveled.

Kai'Ro paused for just a moment to catch his breath. He took another look at the sign called PATH OF LEAST RESISTANCE but then shook his head. With quick strides, he headed up the Heavenly Highway.

THE GATE AND GOODWILL

STORYTELLER: I could tell that Kai'Ro was ready to get to the Gate. He half-jogged down the dirt road until it unexpectedly turned into cracked blacktop. The sun was fading in the sky overhead and the light along the road was growing dimmer.

Kai'Ro kept moving until suddenly, he came up on a long wall that blocked him from going further. The big, thick wooden Gate stood directly in front of him. He pulled on the handle but the huge door wouldn't budge. Then he rapped a large iron knocker and beat the door with the flat of his hand.

GOODWILL: Who goes there?

KAI'RO: It's me, Kai'Ro, from the City of Doom.

GOODWILL: Why do you come to the Gate?

KAI'RO: Man, I'm here to get on that Heavenly Highway so I can get rid of this terrible burden.

GOODWILL: Then we don't have a lot of time, do we?

STORYTELLER: With that, the Gate was thrown open. Before he knew it, a strong arm grabbed Kai'Ro and yanked him inside.

KAI'RO: Yo, take it easy! What'cha grabbin' me for, dawg?

GOODWILL: Sorry, brother, but just beyond this wall is one of Diablo's Towers. He has expert marksmen up there who'd love to snipe a brother dead just before he comes through the Gate. The whole door of this Gate is tore up with bullet holes. I'm surprised you didn't see them.

KAI'RO: (straightening his shirt) Naw, it's gettin' dark. I didn't see the holes, but thanks for pullin' me in. You just surprised me, that's all.

GOODWILL: No big deal. So, you headin' for the Mountain of the Cross?

KAI'RO: Yeah.

GOODWILL: (laughing joyously) This is wonderful news! Aw, man, you just gotta stay with me tonight. We gotta talk.

KAI'RO: I really should keep goin'. I lost some time today, talkin' to the wrong brotha.

GOODWILL: Man, you don't want to get on this Highway in the dark. There's some crazy cats out at night. You can get up early.

KAI'RO: Appreciate it.

STORYTELLER: I could see that Goodwill had a little house just beyond the Gate. Inside he had a small living room with a couch and two chairs. There was a kitchen, a bathroom and a bedroom. You could see all of these things from the front door. Goodwill told Kai'Ro to have a seat. He offered him a sandwich out of the fridge and the two began to talk.

KAI'RO: (in between bites) So, what'cha doin' at this Gate?

GOODWILL: I feel in my spirit that I just gotta help draw people in. You'd be surprised how many people make it all the way to the Gate. Sometimes I can hear them shufflin' their feet on the other side and then just change their minds. Some of 'em reach for the handle and get hit by one of the snipers' bullets. Some get shot dead, and others get hurt so badly they limp home angry and messed up.

The Spirit Himself tugs a lot of sistas and brothas like yourself to the Gate, but it takes a step of faith and courage to really go for it. Know what I mean? I just gotta give some cats that extra tug or push or whatever it takes.

KAI'RO: Like you did with me.

GOODWILL: Exactly. So, you know what you're gettin' in for on this journey?

KAI'RO: Man, I just wanna get rid of this burden. If I can do that, then I'll be straight.

GOODWILL: Yeah, you'll be "straighter," but it ain't over.

KAI'RO: (putting down his sandwich) What'cha mean, it ain't over?

GOODWILL: I mean, it's over for that burden on your back, but the journey itself ain't over. You gotta walk this road all the way to the City of Light. It don't stop until you get there...

KAI'RO: Preacher told me all that. That's where I'm headin', to the City of Light, in case you're wonderin'. But my main thing is to get rid of this burden because it's drivin' me mad, for real.

GOODWILL: Well, you're almost there, dawg. Tell me how you found out 'bout that burden.

KAI'RO: When I was a boy, I used to be up in church every Sunday. Grandma and Moms used to drag me there every week. I sang in the choir, ushered, and all that. I was a pretty good kid. But you know, when I got older, I got mixed up in some things. I started rollin' with some boys that was real hard. I mean, we got into some stuff. We stole stuff from stores. Smoked a little. That's when I started stealin' from Moms. Started hustlin'...got in a lotta fights, homie. Yeah...a whole lotta fights. Started carryin' a piece. I used it a coupl'a times—but don't know if I ever killed nobody.

Man, it kinda all became like one of those blurry dreams, you know? I just remember not feelin' nothin' at all. I'd go to bed at night numb and just stare at the ceiling. I saw two of my boys get shot. One of 'em died and I didn't even cry at his funeral. I was kinda dead myself, I think. Moms used to try and talk to me, and I just wouldn't say nothin' at all.

GOODWILL: Sounds like God was backin' you up against a wall, for real.

KAI'RO: Yeah, it was somethin' like that. Then I moved out of the house when I was seventeen and moved in with my girl, Evangeline. She was good to me. We were doin' all right.

One night, me and two of my boys got arrested for fightin' at a club. I beat up three guys real bad, but I got pretty messed up myself. I was sittin' in a jail cell, mad and hurtin' all over. That's when I met Preacher. He showed up out of nowhere and just talked to me through the bars for like two hours or somethin'.

I tuned him out at first 'cause I didn't like those Holy Roller preachers, but there was somethin' about this guy. His eyes were full of fire. You know, the kinda fire that fighters have. But at the same time, his eyes were full of some kinda peace. He just stared at me and I felt like he was seein' deep into my heart, for real. He told me that I was on a path to death and that God, in His mercy and love, had spared me again and again.

I don't know how he knew, but he listed like three or four things that actually happened to me. And I had never met him before. Preacher told me that God's goodness and kindness would lead me to repentance, but instead I was hardenin' my heart.

He was right, dawg. There were some times when I should have died, for real. Like the time I got in a nasty car wreck when I was real drunk. My car got crushed up on a telephone pole like a Coke can, and I just walked away with hardly a scratch. Then I was at a party one night when some dudes got in a fight and started firin' off shots inside the house. Everybody started runnin.' The cat next to me got dropped . . . found out later he was paralyzed. It was like God was lookin' out for me the whole time, and I just wasn't payin' Him no attention. Lookin' back . . . me survivin' those things was no coincidence.

GOODWILL: You're right. God was screamin' for your attention and tryin' to show you how much He loved you.

KAI'RO: Yeah. Preacher told me that my lifestyle offended God, but he also said that the King loved me and died for me. He told me that my life deserved the price of death, but the King paid that price for me on the Cross.

This cut me deep. I was like "whoa." It made me listen so hard, and I didn't want him to stop talkin' about this stuff. I had heard religion before, but this guy was breakin' down stuff on a whole different level for me. He told me that my city was headed for destruction and that I'd go down with it if I didn't get on this Heavenly Highway.

GOODWILL: So, when'd you notice the burden?

KAI'RO: I don't remember exactly. I mean, I think it had always kinda been there in the back of my mind . . . botherin' me. But somewhere around the time Preacher started talkin' about me offendin' God, I started feelin' weighed down and desperate. I felt like I had to bust out of that jail. I just felt trapped and terrified too.

While I was in there, I talked to my girl about what Preacher said. She just laughed at me every time I brought it up. I asked her if she wanted to go to the Heavenly Highway with me and get rid of her burden too. Evangeline always just looked at me crazy and she'd say, "What burden, boy?" I knew then that I'd have to do somethin', for real, even if it meant goin' by myself. I had to say goodbye to that thug life. So, here I am.

GOODWILL: That's deep, homie. Thanks for sharin' with me. It's funny 'cause almost everybody's got a different story for why they come to the Gate, but everybody's got one thing in common—that doggone burden.

KAI'RO: Can't wait to lose it forever. I know I'll feel so good...

GOODWILL: There are still some struggles you'll be facin' on your way to the Mountain of the Cross. You've got to be careful. Real careful.

KAI'RO: What'cha mean?

GOODWILL: The Heavenly Highway has all kinds of cats on it. Some of them are headin' to the City of Light like you, but a lot of them are just frontin'. They're some treacherous dudes, and they'll pull you off the path real quick—if you aren't careful.

KAI'RO: What'cha mean, frontin'?

GOODWILL: They're imposters, man. They're like wolves in sheep's clothing. They talk a good game, you know? But they don't walk it at all. Some of them are just plain religious. They talk church talk and even wear church clothes, but they stink like the world because that's how they're livin'.

KAI'RO: That used to be me. I mean, that's how I lived until I started feelin' this burden.

GOODWILL: They're a more dangerous animal. Most of these guys know about the burden, but they moved past it. It's like they discovered how to block it out and just move on. They've got hard hearts. When you find out about the burden and then move past it, it's like you've reached a whole new level of evil.

Once the Spirit sticks our heart and we recognize our bad lives, then we can go one of two directions. In your case, man, you said, "Enough is enough." You're headin' to the Cross. A lot of guys just say, "That's all right. I can live with this burden. I can still do my thing." It's tragic, man. It's like they've got a deep hunger for hell. They want hell. And they're gonna get hell too.

KAI'RO: I hear you. I know some guys like that. I don't understand it, dawg. I'm one of those guys who can't live with the fact that somethin's broken. I just gotta fix it. When I heard there was a cure for my burden and my sin problem, I just had to go out and find it.

GOODWILL: (standing up) Be sure to stop by Interpreter's place. You'll run into his house along the way, and he'll be glad to explain some things to you that will help you on your journey.

KAI'RO: That sounds good. I'll definitely look him up.

GOODWILL: Yeah, well, you need to rest. You've got a big day ahead of you tomorrow.

KAI'RO: Sounds good.

CHURCHBOY

STORYTELLER: When Kai'Ro woke up the next morning, he looked better. He and Goodwill had some bacon, eggs and grits for breakfast. They talked for a little bit, but Kai'Ro wanted to get going. So he told Goodwill thanks and then took off onto the road again.

The morning air was cool and Kai'Ro was moving quickly. He walked for a while until he spotted a small white church off to the side of the road. The church was called Church of the Sunday Morning Faithful. The sign said it was run by Pastor Dualist. Kai'Ro squinted his eyes at the sign for a minute but decided to keep going.

After a while, he saw a lanky man leaning against a tree, smoking a Black & Mild. The guy was wearing a red tall-T and a backwards ball cap. He had a large gold chain around his neck with a diamond-studded skull hanging from it. Kai'Ro nodded at the man, hoping he could just pass him by.

CHURCHBOY: What's up, playa?

KAI'RO: What's up?

CHURCHBOY: Hold on, man. Where you goin'?

KAI'RO: I'm headin' to the Mountain of the Cross down the road a ways from here.

CHURCHBOY: (takes a long drag from his cigar) Yeah? That's cool. I'm a religious guy too.

STORYTELLER: I could tell that Kai'Ro wanted to keep moving, but he stopped to give the man a moment of his time.

CHURCHBOY: You prob'ly passed my church back there.

KAI'RO: You go to that Church of the Sunday Morning Faithful?

CHURCHBOY: Yeah, homie. I'm one of the deacons there.

KAI'RO: For real?

CHURCHBOY: Yeah. I've been goin' there my whole life. My girl sings in the choir.

KAI'RO: You married?

CHURCHBOY: (laughing) Naw, dawg. It ain't like that. Can't tie this boy down, for real. I mean, we been livin' together for 'bout three years. But I can't see myself gettin' married, for real.

KAI'RO: And you're a deacon at your church?

CHURCHBOY: Shoot! I preach sometimes. I sing sometimes. I usher. I do it all. I'm up there every Sunday, doin' my thing for the church.

KAI'RO: So, what do you do for a job?

CHURCHBOY: (flicking some ash on the ground) I got a little club I run down the way. It's called Saturday Fire. It's slammin' every Friday and Saturday, dawg. You should see the shorties dancin' up in there. Man, it's off the chain!

KAI'RO: (shaking his head) Naw, I don't do that scene no more.

CHURCHBOY: What'cha talkin' 'bout, playa? Every dude loves a good club where he can meet some ladies and get a little somethin' to drink. What'cha mean, you don't do that scene no more?

KAI'RO: That whole scene is played out, dawg. I mean, I used to be up in the club all the time. I just can't do that no more. That stuff just makes me depressed now. I mean, it's off the chain while I'm there. But when I get home, I just feel empty inside.

CHURCHBOY: (chuckling) Man, that's messed up. How does a guy go home feelin' empty after chillin' with his boys and dancin' with some fine women? That's craaazy, dude!

KAI'RO: Yeah, maybe. I'm tryin' to figure how a dude can go from clubbin' on Saturday night to preachin' a sermon the next morning at his church. That's what I'm tryin' to figure out.

CHURCHBOY: (waving his hand at Kai'Ro) That ain't no big deal. Like I said, I'm religious, man. I do my thing for the church. There ain't nothin' wrong with doin' what I do. You judgin' me or somethin'?

KAI'RO: No, it's not like that. I'm not judgin' you. But from what I've been readin', God will judge you for bein' two-faced. The Word calls what you're doin', *bein' a hypocrite*. And every time that word comes up...some bad stuff follows. I'm just tellin' you that I don't think you can keep up both of those lives forever.

   I mean, I did it for a while myself. But when I started readin' this Book and started listenin' with my heart, I could see that I had a real problem. That's when I started feelin' a real burden on my back. And once I heard how I could get rid of it, I took off on this road I'm on. You ever heard of the Mountain of the Cross?

CHURCHBOY: I mean, I've heard of it. I've never been there, for real, but I believe in it and everything. Pastor Dualist always tells us just to make it to church, keep our tithe comin', and stay away from the really bad stuff. I put somethin' in the plate every Sunday. Ya feel me?

KAI'RO: That's how I was too for a long time, but Preacher told me that I couldn't keep livin' like I was. He said that my life was lost in darkness. And it was, dawg. He said that I could walk in the light, but I couldn't have it both ways. I couldn't keep doin' my thing in the dark and then try to get back in the light on Sunday. He told me that I'd need to get to the Cross where my sins would be forgiven and I could experience Life for the first time, for real. He said that's where I'd find the power in the King to change. That's what I want, and that's where I'm goin'.

CHURCHBOY: I don't like that word *sin*. I mean, who's to really say what it is, for real? I just try to be a good person and get to church. I've never killed nobody, and it ain't like I deal dope or nothin' like that. I mean, we all sin. Don't we? You're no different than me. You sin too.

KAI'RO: I know I do, but I'm sick of it, homie. You don't seem to be sick of it—and it don't seem to bother you. I feel guilt in my soul when I do those old things...why don't you feel no guilt? I just can't live it up six days a week and then try to get religious one day a week. I wanna have the power to change. I believe I'm goin' to find it at the Cross. You should come with me, homie.

CHURCHBOY: Like I said, dude, I don't see the big difference. I go to church and do my best. Ain't nobody perfect. I don't see how I gotta give up certain things in my life and make my life harder and all that. Some of them real religious cats have no fun at all, dawg. It's like they can't do nothin' fun.

KAI'RO: I guess that's where we're different then. I mean, from what I understand, my life is gonna get easier 'cause I'm gonna get rid of this burden and live a Life of freedom. I want freedom, dawg. I'm talkin' 'bout *real* freedom...not just the freedom to do what I want...because that whole life runs dry. I'm talkin' about the freedom from bein' empty and depressed and angry all the time. I want the freedom to live this life the way it's 'sposed to be lived.

I mean, imagine if everybody would obey just one of the Ten Commandments. Like, what if everybody stopped killin'? I mean *everybody,* dawg. Don't you think that would make the world a better place? Don't you think if everybody obeyed that one commandment, it would help us all live a little more the way we're 'sposed to live? I think God has given us rules—not 'cause He wants to take away our joy—but 'cause He wants to protect us from losin' that joy through our own foolishness 'n mistakes. He wants us to find our joy in Him and in followin' Him down the road that He walked when He was on earth.

CHURCHBOY: Yeah. I guess we're just different. I feel like I'm livin' and I'm happy with my life. To each his own, playa. To each his own.

KAI'RO: I used to say that too. We'll see, dawg. I gotta keep movin' on to the Mountain of the Cross. Peace.

CHURCHBOY: We'll see you around. Feel free to swing by my church on Sunday. I think you'll be feelin' it.

KAI'RO: Don't think so, homie. I hope you think about what I said. Peace.

INTERPRETER'S HOUSE

5

STORYTELLER: Kai'Ro waved goodbye to Churchboy and headed on down the road. A little while later, he came to a mailbox that read: "Interpreter." He stopped and stared down the long driveway. There was a big house with large windows. Kai'Ro remembered Goodwill's words and took off down the concrete path until he reached Interpreter's door.

After he knocked, an older man answered promptly. His face was very wrinkled and he had dark brown eyes. When he saw Kai'Ro, the old man smiled.

INTERPRETER: Can I help you, pilgrim?

KAI'RO: Yeah, my name is Kai'Ro, and I was told by Goodwill to stop by and see you. He said that you would show me some things and explain them to me.

INTERPRETER: If you are a traveler in search of wisdom, then you have come to the right place. I'll be happy to show you some things. Please come in.

STORYTELLER: Interpreter stepped aside while Kai'Ro entered the house. I was surprised to see how huge it was. There were many, many rooms and each one had a closed door. Interpreter waved his hand at Kai'Ro to follow him, and they moved together towards a big red door.

INTERPRETER: (opening the door) Come in and let me show you this. I'd like for you to see Patience and Passion.

STORYTELLER: When they went into the room, I saw two boys sitting at different tables. They must have been about eight or nine years old. One of the boys sat quietly at his table looking at a beautiful picture. It was a picture of the ocean, with blue-green waters, shining white sand, and all kinds of tall green palm trees. It was an amazing scene. The kid just looked at it with a big smile and sometimes he'd touch the picture like he was trying to imagine how cool a place like that must really be.

Then I looked at the other boy. Sitting with his head in his hands, he kept rolling his eyes and sighing real loud. He had the same picture as the first boy. But after looking at it for just a few seconds, he pushed it off the table and onto the floor. Every now and then, he'd look up at a clock on the wall and then sigh again. All of a sudden, a fat and dirty looking man came in carrying a big grey bucket of sand. He walked over to the boy and poured it out on the table.

The boy smiled and began playing with the sand. He seemed to be having fun and started building a castle. But every time he got a few parts of it built, another piece would just fall down and he'd have to start all over. I could tell he was getting frustrated because it happened a whole bunch of times. The boy grew more and more angry, but he kept on trying even though it wouldn't work.

Then suddenly, a huge gust of wind blew all of his sand off the table. As it did, a nicely dressed woman with a face like an angel came into the room and walked up to the other boy. Speaking softly, she asked him, "Are you ready to go, my child?" The boy's face lit up. "Are we going here?" he asked excitedly, pointing at his picture. "Yes we are," she said with a smile. Then she took the happy child by the hand and they left together. I looked over at the other boy with his sand scattered all over the floor. He was crying his eyes out.

INTERPRETER: What do you see here, son?

KAI'RO: I'm not sure I understand. I mean, I'm pretty sure that the kid who left is Patience because it was like he was just waiting patiently to get up and go to that beautiful beach. That other boy was just all restless and whinin'. I'm pretty sure he's Passion.

INTERPRETER: You're right about that. Now let's look at these two boys a few years down the road. I think you'll understand better then.

STORYTELLER: The two stepped through a big green door at the back of the room. Immediately, I saw a young man in his early thirties sitting at a large wooden table. Across from him was a beautiful woman. The couple was smiling at each other, and I noticed gold wedding rings on both of their hands. At the table with them were three children. The children were laughing and carrying on in a joyful way. Then the man at the table asked them to be quiet, and they all bowed their heads and prayed. It was a pretty long prayer with many "thank yous" to God for all His blessings and provisions.

When he was finished, they passed around several dishes full of delicious looking meats and greens. There was so much happiness at the table as the family talked and enjoyed each other's company. Every now and then, the man would look up at his wife and just smile or wink at her. There was a lot of love in that room.

INTERPRETER: Come, Kai'Ro, let's look at something else.

STORYTELLER: The two of them left and walked through an old, beat-up door into a dank and musty room that smelled like stale cigarettes and sweat. I saw a young man in the middle of the room, standing there with a big smile on his face. He had on some real baggy jeans and a black baseball cap. The black tall-T he was wearing had a skull and crossbones on the front of it.

Pretty soon, a real scandalous looking girl in a tight red dress walked into the room. They talked for a minute and then started kissing. At the blink of an eye, I saw her disappear into thin air.

From the other side of the room, another girl walked in. She was wearing a short black skirt and a tight sweater. She smiled at him in a real seductive kind of way. Then, just like with the first girl, they started kissing real passionately. Soon she disappeared too.

Another girl came in, and then another, and then another. This went on until I lost count. The next thing I knew, there was a bright flash and I saw the man in the corner of the room smoking with a couple of his homies. There was another flash and I saw him in a different part of the room, drinking something out of a crumpled paper sack. Then there were two more flashes with more girls and kissing.

After yet another flash, I saw the man in the middle of the room with a crazy look on his face. All of a sudden, six children of different ages came into the room. Three of the littlest ones either crawled or walked up to him and were pulling on his pants legs, trying to get him to hold them or play with him. Two slightly older ones just kind of stared at him, wondering if he was going to look at them or even talk to them. The oldest one, a girl, just glared at him with her arms folded across her chest.

In another burst of light, they were gone. The doors in the room opened and most of the different girls that I had seen earlier came back in, yelling and fussing at him. Some of them were screaming at him and demanding their money. Others cursed at him and called him a no-good daddy. A few of them slapped him and hit him in an awful way.

Then there was a final flash, and I saw the man hunched over in the corner of the room with his knees pulled up to his chest. His clothes were all raggedy and he looked skinny and weak. I could tell that he was real sick. He just dropped his head onto his knees and started crying like a baby.

INTERPRETER: Maybe now you understand, son?

KAI'RO: I think so, but why don't you explain it to me a little bit.

INTERPRETER: Both of those little boys in the first room were promised a trip to that amazing beach, and Patience was willing to wait for that promise. In fact, he put so much hope and trust in that promise that he found joy even in the waiting.

But Passion couldn't wait for the promises and delights of God's heavenly Kingdom. He wanted all of his delight now. Since he wanted his pleasure right away, the closest thing he could get was a bucket full of dried-up sand. There's nothing you can do with a bucket of sand.

For a while, he thought it was cool. But once Passion realized he could do nothing with it, he got mad and frustrated. It's sad, but a lot of people trade Heaven and the promises of God's joy for a bucket of lousy sand.

In God's presence, there is fullness of joy; and, at His right hand, there are pleasures forevermore. We have been given an enormous promise for this life and the next. But many reject God's promise and choose to live outside of the King's presence. Even worse, those who are cast from His presence will experience an empty and painful life, as well as eternal punishment in the pit of hell.

KAI'RO: It seems crazy that someone would trade a trip to a place as tight as that one in the picture for a bucket of dried-up sand.

INTERPRETER: Well, it is a form of craziness. It's called a depraved mind, and a lot of people have one. When someone decides to turn their back on God and starts shaking their fist at His Word, He hands them over to their own ways and desires. They don't understand something very important. You see, there's a way that seems right to a man, but in the end it leads to death. When any man is handed over to his own desires and lusts, he finds himself in a terrible place like Passion did.

Now think about the other room where Patience was eating a joyful dinner with his family. You see, Patience waited for the right woman. He got teased a lot growing up, but he trusted in God's commandment to wait until he got married to have sex. Although he was tempted like anyone else, he hung on. He found the girl of his dreams in college, got married and landed a great job. As you saw, God provided him and his wife with three beautiful children. Patience waited and obeyed what God told him to do.

KAI'RO: (in deep thought) Yeah, his beautiful family was sorta like a beautiful beach . . .

INTERPRETER: Now you're starting to get it. Passion had heard God's commands and heard about the promises, but he wanted all of his pleasure immediately. He found a lot of fine women and had a lot of fun times. But as time went on, his life started falling apart. He got a bunch of girls pregnant and got involved in the fleeting pleasures of drugs, drinking and partying.

It was a good time for a short while. But one day he woke up with six kids expecting him to be a daddy, and he wasn't willing or ready to be one. All those girls came to him looking for child support and the man was broke. The drugs and drinking took a toll on his health and the poor guy just wasted away. He missed out on all the promises that Patience waited for to come true.

KAI'RO: (shaking his head) Man, did he ever miss out. That coulda' been me. I was livin' like him, but not no more.

INTERPRETER: Come on. There's more to see.

STORYTELLER: The two men walked into the hallway and Interpreter led Kai'Ro through a thick, brown wooden door. There they watched a young woman out in an open field. She was on her hands and knees digging in the ground when she came upon a great fortune. It was one of the most beautiful and shiny treasures I had ever seen. The woman's face was filled with joy as she gazed at it.

As fast as she could, she got up and raced to her house. I watched as she furiously gathered all her things together. The young lady snatched up a small box of jewelry, all of her CDs, an iPod, her computer, a whole bunch of clothes and some other items. Everything she owned was tossed into boxes and carried down to her car. Then she drove to a large market and sold it all.

Finally, she even traded in her car and got rid of her apartment. With her money clutched tightly in her hand, the young lady walked to a real estate office called Kingdom Property. She gave a man there all the money she held in her hand. Then the man gave her the deed to some property. A huge smile brightened her face and she took off running again back to where the treasure was found. With joy and excitement, she pulled the valuable fortune out of the ground. It was a million times more priceless than any of the things she had sold and given up.

INTERPRETER: This one is not so hard to understand. The treasures of the Kingdom are like the treasure in that field. There, she found true peace, hope and joy. When the young woman found this treasure, she gave up everything that she had in exchange for it. She understood its full value and realized that earthly treasures, such as cars, clothing, jewelry and all of the possessions of this world pale in comparison. How many people have it the other way around?

KAI'RO: Most everybody does.

INTERPRETER: This woman put the treasures of the Kingdom first. Truly, we *all* have to do that if we want to receive the King's best. If we store up our treasures here on earth, then we don't really want the Kingdom. We just want to pretend that we do. Don't be fooled. The treasures of this earth are powerful things that can pull you away, son.

KAI'RO: I feel you.

INTERPRETER: (smiling and putting his hand on Kai'Ro's shoulder) Let's look at something else. Follow me.

STORYTELLER: They walked further down the hall and passed many rooms. Kai'Ro stopped to stare at one of the paintings hanging on a wall.

KAI'RO: What's this painting all about?

INTERPRETER: (smiling) That painting has stopped many travelers. We'll come back and look at it before you leave.

KAI'RO: Cool.

STORYTELLER: Interpreter walked to another door and they went through it. The first thing I saw was an amazing white castle that had towers rising high up into the sky. Giant flags with crosses on them were snapping in the wind. Bright light was bursting from the castle like sun fire.

As I looked down, I saw a gang of angry looking thugs. They each had different words written on their shirts. Some of them were POVERTY, HOPELESSNESS, HUSTLIN', ADDICTION and LUST. With their fists balled up, they glared at a young man with a fierce fire in his eyes. He had on baggy jeans and a wife beater. There was a beat-up Bible in his back pocket and a large silver crucifix swung from the chain on his neck. Between him and the band of thugs, an old man sat at a table with a large open Book.

The young man stepped up to the table and leaned on it, until he was looking the old man straight in the eyes. "You add my name to that list," he said with an unusual boldness. With a pen of golden ink, the man wrote the young man's name down in the Book. "This is an ink that no one can erase," the old man said to him with a smile. "I know, sir," the young man said. Glancing at the thugs on the other side of the table, he added, "And now I gotta go."

Then the determined young warrior took off in a sprint, running hard. He hit that pile of gangbangers like a lightning bolt. They were swinging and hitting at him as hard as they could, but he gave as good as he got. I saw that there was going to be no way they could hold him back. POVERTY grabbed him from behind and ADDICTION punched him three times in the stomach. But the young man struggled and shook himself free. He gave POVERTY such a hard punch to the throat that he never got up again.

He swept ADDICTION'S legs right out from underneath him and then put him in a submission hold until ADDICTION started begging for mercy. LUST, HUSTLIN' and HOPELESSNESS saw their window to strike and they pounced on him like starving cats on a mouse. They were beating on him bad while he was finishing off ADDICTION.

For a minute, it looked like the young warrior might be done for. HOPELESSNESS, in particular, was dropping powerful blows as if he were trying to pound the young man into the ground like a railroad spike. But then, with a great yell, the unwavering young man tossed them off and got back on his feet. With amazingly quick hands, he fired punches into HUS-TLIN' until he dropped to the pavement in a heap.

HOPELESSNESS and LUST remained. HOPELESSNESS was built like a giant, with arms like oil drums. LUST was small and shifty and kept trying to sneak up behind the young man. The three of them circled around for a while with the young warrior in the middle. He had his guard up and, though he was bruised and bleeding, he wouldn't back down. Suddenly, LUST shot in from behind with surprising quickness and gave him a savage punch in the side. The young warrior cried out but spun around and delivered a powerful kick that caused LUST to do a back flip. The wretched thug was knocked out cold.

Now, only HOPELESSNESS stood between the young man and the castle. "Better step off," the fierce warrior shouted. "You ain't so strong now that your friends are gone." HOPE-LESSNESS stood his ground. "I warned you, dawg," the warrior said with a smile. Then he raced towards HOPELESSNESS like a running back who had just busted through the line with nothing but green grass ahead.

HOPELESSNESS took one long, hard swing, but he wasn't quick enough. The young man lit into him like a thunder crack, unleashing a combination of punches and kicks that were so powerful and so furious that HOPELESSNESS buckled up like a folding chair and fell to his knees. The mighty young warrior put his hand on HOPELESSNESS' forehead and pushed the giant over as easy as if he were a balloon.

With all of his enemies fallen, the young man took off running. He ran and ran until he came to the gate of the palace. He hollered at the top of his lungs, "I'm home, Master. Please take me in!" The large drawbridge came down and he hobbled on, totally exhausted. The door was pulled up again and I heard an explosion of cheers and clapping.

INTERPRETER: (with a nod) I think you know what this means, son.

KAI'RO: (grinning) Yeah. I know what this one is all about.

INTERPRETER: This walk that you've chosen is a beast, my son. Many, many things will oppose you and try to destroy you. Some of them won't let up until you make it all the way. It's an everyday struggle, this walk you're on. You press on! Do you hear me?

KAI'RO: Yes, sir. I hear you.

INTERPRETER: Let's look at another room. I want you to meet Backslider and Limping Saint.

STORYTELLER: They walked through a brown door into yet another room. There were two men miserably stuck in some nasty looking mud. They looked hopeless and helpless. Another man dressed in white came walking up to them. "Brothers," he said, "surely you don't want to remain in this mud all of your lives. I can tell you how to get cleaned up and how to get your lives straightened up." He reached forward with a strong hand and pulled them out.

They were led to a small church where a pastor offered them a place to shower and put on fresh clothing. When the two men came out, they were both cleaned up. Afterwards, the pastor read to them from his Bible about how they could be saved if they confessed their sins. Both men nodded that they wanted to do so. Then the man told them about the King and how He died for them and took the blame for all their nasty ways. He told them that they'd have to confess this King as Lord and give their lives over to Him.

Both men bowed their heads and the pastor led them in a prayer. They asked that the King would forgive them and said that they'd follow the King for the rest of their lives. The men prayed for the grace to change their ways. They prayed that the King would help them give up the sinful desires in their hearts and lives—the places where they had made mistakes and fallen into continual sin.

As they were asking for help, I saw that one guy was praying real hard. Tears were streaming down his face and he kept his head bowed towards the ground. The other guy was praying words, but he was just looking around. I could tell that he was just speaking to make himself feel better. When they were both done, the pastor gave them both a Bible and a hug.

Next, the two men walked out and took two different paths. One man fixed his eyes in his Bible as he walked down the path he chose. Sometimes he'd fall down, but he always fell forward. And when he fell, he got up quickly, dusted himself off and then got going again. The further he walked and the more he read, the less he fell, until he hardly fell at all. From some of his difficult and painful falls, he started walking with a little limp. But he never quit moving forward.

The other man started walking on his path the same as the first guy, but it didn't take very long before he lost his Bible on the side of the road. Right away, he started falling down too. But every time he fell, he fell backwards and would take his time getting up. And before long, the white robe that the church gave him was getting real dirty and stained. Soon, he started stumbling and tripping more and more, and sometimes the falls were extremely painful. Finally, he took a really bad spill and tumbled backwards so far that he ended up back in that nasty mud where he started.

INTERPRETER: What do you see here?

KAI'RO: Well, it's obvious that Backslider is the dude who fell back in the mud again. And Limpin' Saint is the dude who kept hobblin' down the road. That part is obvious, but why's he called Limpin' Saint?

INTERPRETER: We have to go back to the beginning of what we saw to understand. Both of those guys came from the same place. They were stuck in the mud of their sins. They heard the Good News and they both took an interest. When Limping Saint heard the Good News, his soul burned for it. On the other hand, *interest* is as far as Backslider really took it. Even in the church when the pastor broke it down for them, Backslider just played along for a while because it sounded good to him and made him feel good to clean up for a while.

When they left that church, one of them left a changed man. Limping Saint took every word that the pastor shared very seriously, and he prayed that prayer with every part of who he was. Yet Limping Saint discovered on the path that he wasn't perfect. No one is *perfect*. That is the reason he kept falling. But he learned that with the power of the Spirit in him, and the Bible in his hands, he had all that he needed to walk that path. That is why he found the strength to get up and keep going when he stumbled and fell.

KAI'RO: Yeah, but he always fell *forward* . . .

INTERPRETER: Exactly! That's the sign of a man making spiritual progress. A righteous man falls seven times, but he keeps getting back up. A growing man *learns* from his mistakes. He prays for forgiveness and experiences the power to change and grow. Everyone walks the path with a limp because of indwelling sin and the damage from the times people give in to it.

Sin will never be fully beaten on this side of Heaven. We all have sin within us that still seeks to take control of our minds, our hearts and our lives—if we're not careful. So, a righteous man falls sometimes. But he gets up and keeps walking and learning. This is a sign of the King's grace in a man's life and a sign that a man is growing in righteousness. A righteous man has no desire to stay down. He wants to see his life look more and more like the King's.

KAI'RO: I get it. Backslider always fell *backwards,* and he took some hard falls. Those looked painful.

INTERPRETER: His walk was like a man going off on a trip up a steep mountain with no shoes, no rope, no water or anything to help him. He's able to get a little ways up the path with a lot of difficulty and scrapes, but after a while he's going to fall. Eventually, he's going to be so weak that he'll fall real hard and give up. Backslider didn't have the Spirit in him and he lost the only guidebook he had when he lost his Bible.

The path of righteousness is not for people who are simply curious. It's for people who are unashamed and willing to go all the way. The King is faithful to give a man what he needs.

He gives that man His Spirit for strength and the light of His Word to show him the way.

STORYTELLER: Interpreter took Kai'Ro down the hallway a little further until they came to a room with a door covered in many different colors.

INTERPRETER: This is a room with great Truth.

STORYTELLER: He opened the door and I saw a large conference room with a big brown table. Seated at the middle of the table was a young man with a bright red T-shirt and a St. Louis cap on his head. He had his hands folded on the table and he looked angry. Then another young man walked into the room wearing a blue tall T-shirt and a throwback Milwaukee hat.

KAI'RO: Uh-oh. Somethin's about to go down here . . .

INTERPRETER: Keep watching, son.

STORYTELLER: The young man in blue sat down across from the kid in red and they glared intensely at each other. Just then, a White kid with a shaved head came in and sat two chairs down from the young man in red. From the tattoos on his arm and neck, he looked like he was from a skinhead gang. A young and beautiful Hispanic girl came in from the other end of the room and sat down. Then a Middle-Eastern man with a long black beard did the same. An old Korean man entered next, followed by a well-dressed Black woman in a business suit.

KAI'RO: This is craaazy! What's happenin' here?

INTERPRETER: You will see soon.

STORYTELLER: A few Latino gangsters and a middle-aged White man in khaki shorts and a polo shirt then entered the room and sat at the table. Next, a girl who looked like she was from Europe came in and sat down as well. Then suddenly the drama began. Several people stood up and started shouting and cursing at each other. Some of them pointed at others around them and angrily waved their arms in the air.

The young man in red tossed his hat on the table and glared at the young man in blue across from him. He threw up some gang signs and the boy in blue threw up his. The White man in khakis shouted and cursed at the Black woman in the business suit and she started screaming back at him.

As those gathered around the table continued to snarl and threaten one another, I noticed that there were several words spray painted on the Wall behind them. In dripping red paint were the words ADAM, IGNORANCE, RACISM, SEGREGATION, and also HATE. Without warning, several of the people in the room actually began to fight. There were punches thrown and even weapons pulled. It was a scary scene.

Suddenly, the projector on the ceiling kicked on and flashed a huge picture of an Old Rugged Cross on the Wall behind them. Everyone stopped fighting and stared silently at the Cross. The picture remained there for one minute. Then with a loud crash like thunder, the entire Wall fell down. For a moment, no one could see because the room was filled with dust.

As it began to clear, I could see a scene on the other side of the Wall. Everyone in the conference room stopped to observe what it was. It was an enormous room filled with millions and millions of people. As far as my eye could see, there were people from all over the world with different colored skin and clothes. They were speaking different languages.

In the far distance at the opposite end of this massive room was a large Throne and there was One seated on it. The light coming from the Throne was blinding, and I couldn't even look at it for long. Those in the conference room looked at each other and then back into the other room.

Pretty soon, the kid in the red shirt walked slowly over the crumbled bricks and into the other room. As he passed over to the other side, his red shirt and red hat were suddenly replaced by a bright white robe. He disappeared into the crowd already gathered inside.

The kid in blue watched in amazement and then he followed. The same thing happened to him. After he went, the others raced into the other room and they too became clothed in the amazingly bright, white robes. Everyone inside began to worship the One seated on the Throne. It was the most beautiful sound I had ever heard.

KAI'RO: Wow. What does this mean?

INTERPRETER: Well, what do you think it means?

KAI'RO: I don't know. I've never before seen a room with so many mismatched kinds of people in it. Whoever decided to bring all those people into that conference room must be a little crazy. There's no way all those different kinds a people are gonna get along, all crammed in a small room like that.

INTERPRETER: The King called that meeting, son. You see, so many people in the world hate other types of people simply because of all the things that they call "differences." It might be differences in skin color or differences in gender. Sometimes it's about what part of the world someone's from and sometimes it's something as small as what part of the block they come from. Some people hate others because of the differences in what they have in their bank accounts. And sometimes it's because of the differences in language.

But really, what causes people to hate each other, to develop racist feelings, and to live segregated lives—is not the differences—it's actually what they all have in common.

KAI'RO: What do you mean?

INTERPRETER: What was the name that you saw on the Wall before it came crashing down?

KAI'RO: It was *ADAM*.

INTERPRETER: That's right. You see, we've all got the same great-great-granddaddy in Adam. You have to go back to the beginning of time when sin first entered the world through Adam. He passed it on to each and every one of us. We're *all* sinners. There's no getting around it. All of the hatred in the world, the racism, and the segregation . . . these are *all* the foul fruit of sin. Sin has a million faces and every one of those faces seeks to separate us from God and to divide us from one another. Sin is a deadly disease that all of us have in common. It tears us all apart and keeps us from really learning how to love one another.

KAI'RO: That's deep. So, the King's blood is the cure?

INTERPRETER: Yes. The common problem of sin is what keeps us all apart, but the common cure that can unite us all together is the blood of the King. The King's blood destroys the work and the effects of sin and builds a bridge between us and God.

On the other hand, apart from the King's saving grace, we are enemies with God. So it is the blood of the King that tears down the walls that divide us from one another. When you give your life to the King, things like race, gender, money, and what part of the block you grew up on no longer become your main form of identity.

You see, in that conference room, everyone was divided from everyone else because of their sinful view of themselves and others around them. The thugs saw only their rag colors. Others could only see the differences in their skin color. And they all hated people who didn't look the same. You also saw some of those people showing hate because they didn't like others at the table who had more or less money than they did. All of them had put up sinful walls and barriers around themselves that didn't allow them to get to know one another.

KAI'RO: That's when the Cross came on the scene.

INTERPRETER: Exactly. Every one of those folks gave their lives to the King. His blood became their new identity. It was like they were all adopted into a new family—the *same* family— with a new Father. They found unity in the King. The walls of race, gender and different neighborhoods came crashing down and they were able to worship together as true brothers and sisters. Those white robes that they all got were a sign of their unity in the King. The King's blood cleansed them and then His righteousness gave them a whole new outfit.

KAI'RO: That's too deep.

INTERPRETER: We sometimes forget that our worship on earth is supposed to imitate the worship going on in Heaven. The Bible tells us that folks from every tribe, tongue and nation are going to be worshiping the King in Heaven. People from every background, every color and every neighborhood are all going to be together doing the very same thing in Heaven. Why can't we try to bring a little of that unity here on earth?

KAI'RO: That's powerful. I think this earth could use a lil' more Heaven these days.

INTERPRETER: (smiling) Yes it could, my son. Now let's go and have a look at that painting that struck you. Then I will see you on your way.

STORYTELLER: The two went back out into the main hallway again and walked until they stopped in front of the big painting. It was a picture of two different scenes. In one scene was a young man who looked a lot like Kai'Ro. The young man was on his knees in front of a large wooden Cross. His head was bowed and his hands were folded.

Behind him was a pile of things. There was a big stack of cash, a bunch of trophies that the young man had won, a fancy looking Benz, a shiny magazine with his face on the front, and a black gun. When Kai'Ro saw the gun, he swallowed hard and looked at Interpreter, but Interpreter didn't notice.

Behind the pile of things was a group of people. There was a beautiful young woman who looked like she might have been Kai'Ro's girl. Some other guys who looked like they were probably his boys were in the picture too. There was also an older woman who looked a lot like his mama standing next to a young boy who looked like his brother. All of them stood away from him at a distance.

KAI'RO: I think I got this side of the picture. That guy is sayin' goodbye to everything the world has to offer. It's like he knows that the Cross has everything he needs and he's turned his back on everything else... looks like he even said goodbye to his family. These are *hard* losses.

INTERPRETER: That's right. The King on that Cross must become your treasure and everything else should be trash in comparison.

KAI'RO: (pointing) But what about this side of the picture? What does it mean?

STORYTELLER: On the other side of the picture, the young man in the painting was on his feet again. He had stepped over the pile of things with his arms wide open. It seemed like he was trying real hard to tell the group of people behind him something real important. Most of the others had their backs turned towards him and some were even walking away with their fingers in their ears. A few of them stuck around, though. I noticed that one of them was the boy who looked like his brother. The kid had a look on his face like he was really listening and thinking.

INTERPRETER: (looking thoughtfully at Kai'Ro) Son, once you find yourself at the Cross, the Master is going to call you to go back...

KAI'RO: (raising his voice) Back to the City of Doom?

INTERPRETER: Maybe. I can't really say. *Going back* sometimes means going back to where you came from. Sometimes it doesn't. Either way, you're going to receive your marching orders.

KAI'RO: I don't get it.

INTERPRETER: You won't fully get this until you meet the Arms Dealer. There you'll receive your weapons and you'll also receive your marching orders.

KAI'RO: *Marching* orders?

INTERPRETER: It's as I said. Later, you'll understand more clearly. Now, son, it's time for you to get going. You are about to make the most important decision of your life.

KAI'RO: I'm ready. Thanks for your time, sir. I learned a lot here today.

INTERPRETER: There is much more to learn, son. You are just beginning. Keep your mind open to knowledge and your heart open to wisdom. The King will surely give it to you.

STORYTELLER: The two of them walked to the front door. Kai'Ro thanked Interpreter, shook his hand, and took off back onto the Heavenly Highway.

BIRDVILLE

6

STORYTELLER: After leaving Interpreter's house, Kai'Ro came quickly upon a town called Birdville. The first thing he noticed was a black and yellow flag flapping from a pole. On the flag was a picture of three large birds gobbling up a bunch of scattered seeds on the ground. He had no idea what to expect.

Just beyond the town, he could see a hill. On top of the hill stood a wooden Cross.

Once he figured out that it was the only way to reach the hill, he took a deep breath and entered the town. There were a bunch of stores on either side of the street with names like "Confused Coffee Shop" and "Happy Living Bookstore." In the windows of the stores were blurry posters advertising things that Kai'Ro couldn't understand. A few men and women moved along the sidewalk, but they hardly looked at him as he moved past them.

Kai'Ro stopped for a minute when he noticed that everyone was wearing the same kind of strange, black slim-rimmed glasses. I could see that he was growing concerned. He saw some more places with names like "Love My Body Gym" and "Mo Money School of Wild Living." There were lots of people moving in and out of the buildings.

At the very center of town was a huge factory with big puffs of grey smoke coming out of the dirty stacks. The factory was called "Clouded Vision Eye Glasses." There were rows and rows of eighteen-wheelers in the main parking lot, and several trucks left the factory, rumbling past Kai'Ro down the street. On the side of the building was the same logo I saw on the flag with the birds and seeds. Across the street from the factory was a nice looking hotel called "Pilgrim Trap." The flashy sign read: "Vacancy."

KAI'RO: (to himself) What kinda' place is *this?* Why is this town right here at the foot of the Cross?

STORYTELLER: Just then, a tall man in a black suit came out of a tinted office complex next to the factory. Spotting Kai'Ro, he hollered at him. He was wearing the same kind of glasses as everyone else.

BLINDMAN: Where are you going, son? You aren't about to go up that mountain there, are you?

KAI'RO: That's why I'm here. Who're you?

BLINDMAN: I'm Blindman. This is my factory. I saw you through the window and had to come out and stop you.

KAI'RO: What'cha mean, stop me? I've already come this far. I don't think you can stop me.

BLINDMAN: Don't be foolish, son. That whole trip up there isn't necessary. So many people think it is, but it isn't. Look around you. We've got ourselves a thriving town here in Birdville. This town was founded a long time ago to spare people the trouble of going up that mountain and getting disappointed. Besides, look at the path up that mountain. It's almost impossible.

STORYTELLER: I looked at the mountain as Kai'Ro checked it out himself. There was a very noticeable path that appeared steep, but it was clearly a path that anyone could climb up if they really wanted to.

KAI'RO: I don't get it...

BLINDMAN: Look at that hill you're about to climb. Have you ever tried to climb something so dangerous before?

KAI'RO: (looking up at the hill) First of all, man, it doesn't look that high or dangerous to me. Besides that, I can see the Cross up there at the top right now. It looks amazin'. I'm sure you can see that it's worth the trip.

BLINDMAN: No. Sorry, son. I don't see anything except a ridiculously tall hill.

KAI'RO: I don't understand . . .

BLINDMAN: Exactly. That's why I'm here to help, son. I'm here to provide you with some understanding and some clear sight. Whoever told you to go up there has filled your head with a bunch of nonsense. Look at me. You don't need to do it, son. There is nothing ahead of you but a long, hard journey filled with frustration.

KAI'RO: I don't think you understand. I've got a real burden on my back. It's a burden of sin and a guilty conscience. I'm gonna go up there and get rid of it.

BLINDMAN: (with a stern face) I'm older than you, young man, and I've been here a long, long time. I know more than you. Who are you to talk to me about understanding? That burden has nothing to do with sin and a guilty conscience. It has everything to do with a troubled mind, because someone put thoughts in there that made you feel bad about yourself. Look around you for a minute. Do you see anyone who looks guilty or even troubled?

STORYTELLER: Kai'Ro took a moment to look at some of the people walking the streets. No one looked that bothered. They just moved around from store to store and place to place like any normal person would. He turned back to Blindman and shrugged his shoulders.

BLINDMAN: Son, you don't see correctly yet. Once you see, you'll understand. You need a pair of these glasses. I should have a pair right here.

STORYTELLER: Blindman reached into his pockets and seemed to get real frustrated when he couldn't find a pair.

BLINDMAN: Tell you what, son. (pointing) See the Pure Sight Vision Center over there across the street? I'll take you there myself and we'll get you what you need. You'll see a lot better after that. Here, I'll go with you. We'll get you the exact pair.

STORYTELLER: Kai'Ro looked at where the man was pointing and saw the *Clouded* Vision Center. He looked confused.

KAI'RO: Man, you must be pointin' to the *Clouded* Vision Center over there, 'cause I don't see no *Pure Sight* Vision Center.

BLINDMAN: It's right there, son. Look!

KAI'RO: Yeah, I'm lookin' right there. That sign doesn't say "Pure Sight Vision Center."

BLINDMAN: Wow, your sight is worse than I thought. The vision center is right next to the Holy Living Bookstore right there.

KAI'RO: You mean the *Happy* Living Bookstore?

BLINDMAN: Okay, boy, now you're just being hardheaded. I've been in Birdville all my life, and I've hardly met anyone with a problem as bad as yours.

KAI'RO: (raising his eyebrow) Look, man. I don't know what kind of joke you're tryin' to play on me, but it ain't funny. You're accusin' me of bein' blind and hardheaded. I know I can read, man! Quit playin'.

BLINDMAN: (with a wave of his hand) Son, do you see all of these trucks leaving the factory here? I have hundreds of trucks pulling out of here every day, delivering these glasses and giving sight to people all over the world. There's a lot of people who just don't understand at all. People just like you. Providing people with sight is a legitimate business. This town has been giving people sight longer than anyone can really remember. The only joke in town is you, boy!

STORYTELLER: Just then, Blindman had a determined look appear on his face. He pulled off his glasses and handed them to Kai'Ro.

BLINDMAN: Here, try these. You'll see what I mean when you put them on. Go ahead. Try them on and then take a look at that hill you're headed for.

STORYTELLER: Kai'Ro appeared doubtful, but he decided to give them a try. Cautiously, he put the glasses on and turned to look at the hill. Immediately, he looked shocked.

KAI'RO: Man, *where's* the Cross? Where's the Cross?! I don't see nothin'! Where'd it go? Man, what's goin' on here?

STORYTELLER: Kai'Ro ripped the glasses off his face and shoved them back into Blindman's hands.

KAI'RO: Those glasses are evil, dawg! Get those things away from me! I couldn't see a thing with those glasses on. They made the Cross disappear. This whole town is an evil place. I need to get outta here now!

STORYTELLER: As Kai'Ro began shouting, some of the other people stopped to see what was going on. Some of them closed in around him.

BLINDMAN: Son, you need to calm down. You've got some serious problems and we can help you, if you'll just let us. Once you let us help you see, then you'll understand . . .

KAI'RO: Naw, man, you need the help. *All ya'll need some help.* Can't you see that you're all blind? Don't you understand what I'm sayin'? Ya'll have been robbed of your sight and your understandin'. You need to get rid of those glasses, man, for real.

Those things are so messed up! Someone needs to shut that factory down! Look what you're doin' to everybody. None of these people can see! You've got 'em all fooled.

(Turning to the crowd) Don't ya'll get it? These glasses have robbed you of understandin'! You live in a town right here by the Cross and yet none of ya'll can even see how close to salvation you actually are! Don't ya care? This man and these glasses are blindin' you! Take those doggone things off of your face and come with me.

BLINDMAN: (angrily) *You* don't understand. Do you, son? Those glasses give all of us the ability to see. There's nothing messed up in this town but your eyes! You can't see! That's why I'm trying so hard to get you to the vision center. Once you own a pair of these glasses, it will all make sense. You'll understand that you're wrong and you'll finally begin to see. Most everyone here was sort of like you at one point. Stop any one of these people and ask them how they feel. They'll tell you how wonderful they feel.

KAI'RO: No. I'm not talkin' to no one, no more. This place is craaazy! I'm headin' up that hill and leavin' this place behind forever!

STORYTELLER: Kai'Ro turned and ran as fast as he could down the street, leaving Blindman and the others behind. He ran hard and never looked back.

THE MOUNTAIN OF THE CROSS

STORYTELLER: As Kai'Ro moved away from the city and towards the hill, he discovered that the path was protected on both sides by a mighty Wall. The Wall was called SALVATION. From far away, the hill looked a lot like a mountain. But up close it seemed a lot smaller.

When Kai'Ro reached the bottom of the hill, he stopped to look at an old wooden sign that read, "Come to me, all who labor and are heavy burdened, and I will give you rest." I could see tears forming in Kai'Ro's eyes as he read that sign. And I could also see that he was struggling under the weight of his burden.

KAI'RO: (encouraging himself) C'mon! You can do this thing. The hope for your soul is at that Cross. All the pain, guilt and drama end there. All the peace, relief and true Life begin there.

STORYTELLER: He started to climb up the hill running at first, but his burden made it hard for him. Kai'Ro stumbled a couple of times but kept getting up. I could tell that he was desperate. The burden got heavier as he drew closer to the Cross. It weighed down on him like a giant boulder. He dropped to his knees as the burden started to pull him backwards.

KAI'RO: (crying out in desperation) This burden is going to crush me! I don't think I can make it to the top! All my sins ... they're just too much...I don't even know if the Cross is strong enough to break the bonds of this burden...I don't know if the King can really take away all the mess and mistakes in my life. They're just too nasty and too foul.

STORYTELLER: Kai'Ro was crawling like a desperate man groping through a desert in search of water. For a moment, it looked as though he could go no further. His arms and legs were shaking under the tremendous weight. His head was bowed because the power of the burden left him broken and nearly hopeless.

Then, just as he came to a point where he could go no further, I saw two small birds land on his shoulder. On one of the bird's wings was the word GRACE and on the other bird was the word REDEMPTION. These two birds gently started to peck away at the straps holding his burden. One of the straps eventually snapped with a loud crack. As it did, I saw a glimmer of renewed Life begin to fill Kai'Ro's body. I saw strength come to his limbs. He was able to slowly rise to his feet again and continue on.

To the side of the path was an open grave. Kai'Ro looked at it for a minute but just kept going. Past the open grave he spotted the old wooden Cross. And as he gazed at it, the burden on his back tumbled off, bounced down the path, fell into the open grave and then disappeared from sight. Kai'Ro fell on his knees at the foot of the Cross and his shoulders were shaking because he was crying so hard. At that moment, three Visitors who looked like angelic beings appeared and placed their hands upon him.

VISITOR ONE: Rise to your feet, Kai'Ro. You are a new creation. The old has gone and the new has come. You do not need to be ashamed, for your King is not ashamed of you. He welcomes you to His City of Light, and He adopts you as His son.

VISITOR TWO: Clothe yourself in righteousness.

STORYTELLER: The second Visitor took away Kai'Ro's dirty rags and gave him a fresh white tall-T, some clean jeans and new tennis shoes. Then the third Visitor put a mark of oil on his right cheek and handed him a small Scroll that was held together with a golden seal.

VISITOR THREE: Take this Scroll and give it to he who guards the Gate at the City of Light. Keep it with you always, for the King will bid you welcome.

VISITOR ONE: Do you know what your name means, son?

KAI'RO: My mom never really said.

VISITOR TWO: It's an ancient name with tremendous historical significance. From the early days of the church, the Chi-Rho was a symbol for the follower of the King. In fact, it was really a symbol for the King Himself.

KAI'RO: What'cha mean?

VISITOR THREE: The ancient Greek letter "chi" and the letter "rho" were the first two letters in the King's name, *Christos*. The early church believers combined those first two letters into the unique symbol "☧".

This is the symbol that I have placed on your face. It is a mark for you to go by as a follower of the King. But it is also *your name.*

KAI'RO: I guess my mom kinda blessed me with a name that would fulfill my destiny or somethin'.

VISITOR ONE: The King had your destiny laid out from the beginning of time, my child. Your name is special and now you must learn in obedience to walk in it.

STORYTELLER: As quickly as they came, they disappeared. Kai'Ro was left alone at the top of the hill. With his face full of joy, he tucked the Scroll into his back pocket and started back down the other side of the hill.

As soon as he reached the bottom, two guys jumped over the Wall along the side of the path. They both looked surprised when they saw Kai'Ro.

KAI'RO: Yo, where'd you two come from?

E.Z. GLIDE: Me and my man, 2-Face, came from the town of Prideopolis. We're on our way to the City of Light.

KAI'RO: Yeah? You skipped the Gate, dawg. You can't just jump the Wall like that.

2-FACE: Look, for those of us in Prideopolis, it's way too far to backtrack like that and go through the Gate. You took your way through the Gate, and we took ours by hopping over the Wall. What's the big deal?

KAI'RO: The King said that guys like you are thieves who come sneakin' over the fence, and that ain't gonna work.

E.Z. GLIDE: You don't need to worry about us, playa'. We've got our thing figured out, fo sho! Looks like you got on some slick clean T-shirt. Did somebody give it to you to cover up you being naked or somethin'? What's that all about?

KAI'RO: These clean clothes were given to me by the King of the Place where I'm goin'. Yeah, it's to cover my nakedness, and I'm thankful for these clothes. Where's your Scroll? Where's your proof that you came by the way of the Cross, dude? You got nothin' to prove that you're for real. You two are gonna be turned away. You need to go by the way of the Gate. There is no other Way.

2-FACE: (laughing) Look, dawg, I don't even know you. You got your little religious spin and everything, and that's cool for you. But we got our plan too.

KAI'RO: I'm not playin'. You two are foolin' yourselves big time. I came in under the King's directions, but you two came on this

Highway followin' your own dreams. And when you get there, you're gonna get turned away without His mercy.

E.Z. GLIDE: Look, man, we're on the same Way as you. We follow the Law and the Customs of the King real good. Prob'ly even *better* than you. I don't think you get it, homie.

KAI'RO: Followin' the Law and Customs of the King is a good thing, but that ain't goin' to save you in the end. You gotta come by the Gate. How many more times do I have to say that, dude? My King is goin' to recognize me because I got His clothes on. I got His mark on me. And I got His Scroll in my pocket. That doggone burden I've had all my life fell tumblin' off at the foot of the Cross. I'm the King's son now, for real.

STORYTELLER: E.Z. Glide and 2-Face burst into laughter, pointing at Kai'Ro. The two of them walked on, with Kai'Ro ahead just a few steps. From time to time, they would point at Kai'Ro and crack on him. He never said anything other than muttering a few words to encourage himself. Eventually, they came to a hill called DIFFICULTY. There was a refreshing stream of cold water flowing in front of the hill and two easier looking paths going around it.

Before beginning up the hill, Kai'Ro sat down to get a drink from the cold waters. But the other two dudes split up, each to take a different road. Trying to avoid DIFFICULTY, they thought that their paths would cross again on the other side of that tall hill. 2-Face took a path called DESPAIR that disappeared into a dark and dense wooded area. E.Z. Glide took a path called DESTRUCTION that led him into some deep mountains. In those mountains, he took a hard fall and couldn't get up again. No one would ever be able to find him.

Kai'Ro went on his way straight up DIFFICULTY. It was a struggle. He started off strong, but after a while he had to stoop over and use his hands because the hill was so steep. About half way up, he grew tired and was breathing real hard.

Not a minute too soon, he came across a little shelter for rest. It had a roof that gave travelers like him some much needed shade.

KAI'RO: (to himself) This looks like a good place to chill for a bit. I'm so tired. Maybe I could just rest for a minute or two...

STORYTELLER: Kai'Ro sat on the ground and leaned up against one of the poles that supported the roof. Without even trying, he fell asleep real fast. He was there for quite a while, resting and snoring. Then all of a sudden, he woke up with a jump.

KAI'RO: (said to himself) Aw, man, the desire of the sluggard kills him, for his hands refuse to labor!

STORYTELLER: Kai'Ro got up quickly and was very mad at himself. The sun had started to dip in the sky, and he knew that he had wasted too much time.

KAI'RO: I'm supposed to run with endurance this race that is set before me. I'm a fool! I been sleepin' in the shade when I shoulda been on my way. Can't believe I did that!

STORYTELLER: Continuing to climb hard for quite a while, he was almost at the top. Then he reached into his back pocket because he wanted to look at his Scroll for some encouragement. Instantly, he realized that it was gone! Kai'Ro was so mad and so scared that he almost started crying. He looked to his left and then to his right but the Scroll wasn't there. Just about frantic with worry, he checked all of his pockets.

KAI'RO: (to himself) Kai'Ro, you been foolish. Now you've lost the most important thing you've got. If you messed up this bad so early in your trip, how are you ever gonna finish this thing?

STORYTELLER: There was still a little light left on the path. So Kai'Ro took off back down DIFFICULTY again, looking everywhere as he walked along the path. The further back he went, the madder he got at himself. It angered him so, until he was almost tempted to start cursing again. The Scroll was nowhere to be found. After a while, he made it back to the covered rest area where he fell asleep. It was almost too dark to see. And so he got down on his hands and knees, reaching around on the ground for his Scroll.

KAI'RO: Man, if I lost it, then what am I goin' to do? God, please let me find this thing . . .

STORYTELLER: Just when he was about to lose all hope, his hand fell on his Scroll. He jumped up and shouted! Kai'Ro was so overjoyed because he had found his Scroll that he took off back up the hill with new strength and purpose. He made it to the top again in half the time it took him earlier.

At the top of the hill, there was level ground again. A short way down the path, he could see the lights of a town. Now that it was dark, he was hoping to find a place to sleep for the night. Hurrying quickly, he came to the edge of the town. The sign along the side of the road read "Rock City: Suffer No Longer."

KAI'RO: (to himself) What kinda place is *this*?

STORYTELLER: Kai'Ro looked unsure about this city, but there were lights down the main street. It was called FALL AWAY AVENUE. There were a few people hanging out in front of a restaurant. They watched Kai'Ro as he started passing by.

KAI'RO: How's it goin'?

TURNBACK JACK: It's good. Where you headin' to?

KAI'RO: I'm on my way to the City of Light.

TURNBACK JACK: Well, you might as well park it here, homie. You don't wanna go up that way any further.

KAI'RO: Yeah? Why's that?

SHIFTY: There's danger up that way. There's all kinda hard things down that road.

KAI'RO: Everyone knows that. That doesn't mean I'm gonna stop here. I'm headin' on to the City of Light. There's no way I'm goin' to lose my burden and then just call it quits like that.

TURNBACK JACK: I had the same thoughts 'bout a year ago. I was headin' up that way. But there's a big ol' house not too far down the path and they got these two crazy, big red-nosed pits there, dawg. They're right up on the path. There was no way I was gonna risk that. Not for real.

KAI'RO: The King promised anyone who followed after Him that there'd be trials and suffering. I mean, I think everybody knows that.

SHIFTY: We'll see. I never even made it to the big house like TJ here. I got just a ways down the road and there was a bunch of dudes that clowned on me so bad. They made fun of my clothes, my mark and everything. I tried to talk to them a little. But then, they got loud and one of them boys even slapped me.

I was thinkin' to myself, "Naw, I didn't sign up to get slapped around like that." So, I headed back and moved to Rock City. There's a lot of folks here that found this place to be much safer. We still believe in the King and everything, but we ain't really interested in walkin' down that road of suffering.

KAI'RO: But the King said that if we weren't willin' to pick up our cross and follow after Him, then there was no point in even botherin' with Him. I don't think you can really say you believe in Him, if you ain't willin' to follow after Him.

TURNBACK JACK: Man, look here. I've had enough drama in my life. I grew up in a bad home with a no good dad and a dead-beat mom. So I took to the streets and lived the street life. You feel me? I decided to believe in the King to leave all that drama behind. I didn't decide to believe in Him so that I could have more drama. You craaazy? Shoot! Rock City is where it's at. We left the nonsense behind, and we ain't goin' to find no more nonsense either.

SHIFTY: We'll wait right here, doin' our thing until the King comes back like He said He would. He'll find us here and it'll all be straight.

KAI'RO: I don't think ya'll get it. You don't understand, for real. I had drama in my life too, and I left it behind in order to lose the burden of my sin. But the King didn't just wanna make me feel better. Trust me, man, I feel better than I've ever felt in my life. But He also told me to follow after Him—and that's what I'm doin'. Come whatever, it don't matter. I'm in this thing till the end.

TURNBACK JACK: Then go for it, dawg. When you see those pits, you'll be runnin' back here just like everybody else does. We ain't here to clown on you, man. We're just tryin' to let you know that Rock City is where it's at. You ain't gotta head down a road full of thugs, beasts and suffering.

KAI'RO: I'm not comin' back through here, and I hope that my courage will inspire some of ya'll to follow after me. You're wastin' your life droppin' out of the race like ya'll doin'. You're goin' to find yourselves disqualified at the end and it'll be sad. Ya'll need to bounce outta this joint and come with me.

TURNBACK JACK: You won't be comin' back. And it won't be because you made it somewhere further—but because you'll be dead. There've been a few cats who made it past the pits somehow. But they came back all scared, talkin' 'bout demons and persecutions. One dude even said there's a whole city out there where they actually thrash followers of the King and put some of 'em to death. No thanks, dude. I'm waitin' right here.

KAI'RO: Then you wait for nothin', man, because no one's comin' for you. When the King comes back, your lamps will be out of oil and you'll miss Him. I wish you'd listen to me and come with me.

SHIFTY: There was another guy like you who passed through here earlier this morning. He wouldn't listen to us either. Maybe you'll find him or what's left of him up there, if you hurry.

KAI'RO: For real? Then I'm out.

THE ARMS DEALER

8

STORYTELLER: Kai'Ro said bye to Turnback Jack and Shifty and moved quickly through what was left of Rock City. He was glad to leave such a pathetic place behind. The words about the pits scared him some, though. It was dark and he knew that he'd have no chance against them.

He moved on for a while, until he saw a big flashing sign along the side of the road. The sign read: "Thorn Town" and it had a bright gold arrow pointing to a side path. On the sign there were pictures of pimped-out cars with chrome wheels, gorgeous looking girls and mountains of cash.

Kai'Ro stopped to stare at it for a while. He read the slogan at the bottom: *Fame and Fortune Just Around the Corner.* Then he said to himself, "Don't store up treasure for yourself where moth and rust destroy and where thieves break in and steal." Next he pulled out his Scroll to get some much needed support. When he did that, the Spirit of the King gripped him and gave him the strength to move on.

A short way down the path, he spotted a large house just like the guys in Rock City had told him. He moved closer until he heard the sound of loud barking. In the path just ahead of the house, he spotted the two huge pit bulls. They were much bigger than normal and almost looked like mutants. One had a large tag with the name LOCKJAW on it and the other was named BONECRUNCHER. Kai'Ro started shaking. He didn't know if they had seen him yet.

KAI'RO: (to himself) Aw, shoot! Those dogs are right in my way. There's nowhere else to go. I either gotta try to sneak past them, or I gotta go back and face those guys again.

STORYTELLER: Kai'Ro stood there for a while just trembling in the shadows. He looked and felt terrible. Finally, he took two steps forward and then one step backwards, like he couldn't make up his mind. To his relief, someone opened up a window at the top of the house and saw him.

KEEPER: Hey, down there! What are you doing?

KAI'RO: I'm makin' my way down the Heavenly Highway, but there's two pits out here who won't let me go any further.

KEEPER: Don't worry about those dogs, boy. They're on chains and they can't reach you, if you stay to the middle of the path.

KAI'RO: For real? I dunno, man.

KEEPER: Trust me. Stick to the path. Come in and you can stay here tonight. It's no good for you to be out on the Highway in the dark.

STORYTELLER: Kai'Ro took a few careful steps forward until the pits were so close that he could hear them breathing. From the light of the house, he could see that they were both chained up like the man in the house had said. He was encouraged and walked quickly up to the door. One of the pits growled again and Kai'Ro jumped up on the porch and started beating on the door.

KEEPER: (opening the door a crack) Where are you from?

KAI'RO: I'm Kai'Ro from the City of Doom.

KEEPER: And how'd you get here?

KAI'RO: I came through the Gate, and just this morning made it to the Mountain of the Cross. I lost my burden there. Just a few minutes ago, I went through Rock City back there...

KEEPER: You sound like you are a true pilgrim. Come in.

STORYTELLER: Kai'Ro stepped into the house. He was relieved to be in a warm place and safely away from the dogs.

KEEPER: We're just about to have dinner. You're welcome to join me and the girls.

KAI'RO: Girls?

KEEPER: Yes. My two daughters, Purity and Peaceful.

STORYTELLER: The Keeper led him into a large dining room. There were two beautiful young girls setting the table. Dressed nicely in long colorful dresses, they looked at Kai'Ro with kind smiles.

PURITY: Hello. Will you be joining us for dinner?

KAI'RO: If I can, I'd love to eat with ya'll.

PURITY: Are you a pilgrim on the King's Highway?

KAI'RO: Yeah. I am.

PEACEFUL: Then please sit down and tell us about your journey so far.

STORYTELLER: The four of them sat down to some delicious food. The girls had cooked fried chicken, collards, potatoes and macaroni and cheese. While they ate, Kai'Ro told them all about his City of Doom. He talked about how he met Preacher and how the man of God explained the problem of sin to him. Kai'Ro told how he left town with Follower and Quitter and how they abandoned him at the Swamp of Despair. He shared with them his conversations with Goodwill, with Blindman in Birdville, and with many of the travelers he met along the way.

They listened to him for a long time without interrupting. When he finished, one of the girls spoke to him.

PURITY: Did you have a wife back in your city?

KAI'RO: No. I mean, I wanted to marry my girl, Evangeline. We just hadn't done it yet.

PEACEFUL: Didn't you tell her about the Heavenly Highway?

KAI'RO: We talked about it a lot. She'd always just laugh and tell me that I was gettin' religious on her.

PURITY: Did you feel like your new passion for the Heavenly Highway affected your relationship?

KAI'RO: Yeah. I loved Evangeline so much, but I started feelin' like our relationship was wrong. I couldn't keep livin' with her like we were doin'.

PEACEFUL: And, did you tell her that?

KAI'RO: Yeah, I told her. She got mad. She couldn't understand it. It was like we were on two different planets or somethin'. I begged her to listen to what was goin' on in my heart, but she just said that she didn't feel what I was feelin'.

PURITY: Didn't you tell her about sin and that sin would destroy her if she wasn't willing to change?

KAI'RO: I told her that sin would destroy us both. I even told her that our sin would kill our relationship eventually, but she just got madder and madder. She said that I was judgin' her and told me that I was in no place to be her judge. I said that God was our Judge and that we'd broken all His laws. I tried to warn her that we were in terrible trouble unless we made some real changes. I explained to her that we had to get on the Heavenly Highway and that the King would give us grace and forgive us for what we'd done. When I said that, she just stared at me and didn't say nothin'. I knew then that I'd have to go without her. So, that's what I've done.

PEACEFUL: You have made a very hard decision, but you've made a good one. As the King said, you must hate your father and your mother in comparison to your love for Him. Otherwise, you are not worthy to be His disciple. You have chosen Life. And your decision will not leave her unchanged if she truly loves you, as it sounds like she does. We must pray that she will follow after you.

KAI'RO: I pray it every day.

KEEPER: Thank you for sharing your story with us, son. You have taken bold steps that most people are unwilling to make. A beautiful girl, a stack of cash, or any flashy thing can keep a man or woman from following the King. Tell me something, did you come by Thorn Town?

KAI'RO: No, but I saw the sign. The sign was tight, I'm not gonna lie.

KEEPER: Well, it's good that you did not visit. Many travelers toss in their towel there.

KAI'RO: Why's that?

KEEPER: Thorn Town is a place that makes a lot of promises. People go there in search of fame, fortune and all kinds of pleasure. For a while, the town gives what it promises. They've got girls and a lot of ways to make quick cash. Some people go there and actually make it big. But like a thorny weed, the town chokes the life out of them. Whatever passion and hope they found at the Cross they exchange for the goods of the city. It's like the hope of the City of Light just gets strangled and dies.

Thorn Town is one of Diablo's greatest cities and one of his greatest traps. Hardly any go there and come back because of its evil power. There are few things more destructive to the soul than a strong love for the pleasures and power of this world.

KAI'RO: I feel you. I'm glad I pressed on.

KEEPER: As are we. Tomorrow morning I will take you to the Arms Dealer. He will give you what you need for the remainder of this journey.

KAI'RO: Like what?

KEEPER: All of the King's travelers need to get armed for the battles ahead. There will be many. And without the Armor, you could easily be overcome.

KAI'RO: Well, I'm up for any help that I can get on this trip. Did another guy pass this way today? Some of the cats back in Rock City said a guy went through there this morning. After what you said, I hope he didn't stop off at Thorn Town.

KEEPER: Yes, a man named Phanatik came by around noon today. He ate with us and then stopped off at the Arms Dealer. This is a very special man. I hope that you can catch up with him tomorrow.

KAI'RO: Did you say Phanatik? I know him. He's from my city! This is great news! I'm goin' to have to bust it tomorrow, if I'm goin' to catch him.

KEEPER: I pray that you overtake him. Come with me and I'll show you to your room.

STORYTELLER: Kai'Ro went to his room and slept hard after his long day. He woke up the next morning feeling strong and ready to go. After a quick breakfast, he followed the Keeper down the path to a stone house with two long swords mounted above the door. The Keeper knocked on the door and a huge man answered it. He had on a bright white wife beater and his arms were nearly as big as Kai'Ro's waist. Kai'Ro just stood there and stared.

ARMS DEALER: Well, what we got here, Keeper? He another traveler?

KEEPER: Yes. This is Kai'Ro from the City of Doom. He's in need of some Armor.

ARMS DEALER: Well then, he's in the right place, ain't he? Come on in.

KAI'RO: Don't you hate guys like me?

ARMS DEALER: Huh? Ohh...you must be referrin' to this tattoo I got on my arm here. Yeah, I used to hate guys like you. Fact is...I used to hate a lot of folks. Not no more, though. This tattoo is a symbol from my past and a part of me that I ain't too proud of. When I gave my life to the King, He took all that hate just right outta me, man. The art on my arm is kinda like a scar of who I once was, but I ain't like that no more. The King made me a new man. When I get my new body in glory, the tattoo'll be gone for good. But I want you to know that I got no ill feelin's towards you or nothin'.

KAI'RO: Guess we all kinda got scars from our past.

STORYTELLER: When Kai'Ro went into the house, it was much bigger than he imagined. There were pieces of Armor everywhere—helmets, shields and swords of all sizes. There were so many that it looked like the Arms Dealer could give some to everyone in the world if they wanted it. Judging by the big fires going, he was obviously making more.

ARMS DEALER: Come over here and I'll git you what you need. But before I git you set up, you need to give me a little somethin', don't you?

STORYTELLER: The Arms Dealer smiled and winked at Kai'Ro.

KAI'RO: What'cha mean?

ARMS DEALER: Now that you're a part of the King's army, you'll be doin' battle in a different kinda way. Yer weapons from the City of Doom ain't no good in this battle.

STORYTELLER: Kai'Ro suddenly looked a little embarrassed. He took off his backpack and unzipped it. Pulling out his shiny black gun, he handed it to the Arms Dealer.

KAI'RO: That thing got me out of a lot of jams back where I came from.

ARMS DEALER: The weapons of the world are for killin'. Yer no longer in a fight 'gainst flesh and blood, but 'gainst much darker and more powerful enemies. Guns and bullets ain't gonna do nothin' 'gainst them.

KAI'RO: What'cha mean? I've never seen anyone who can stop a bullet.

ARMS DEALER: That may be true, but you'll be fightin' 'gainst the forces of evil now. They ain't 'fraid of no bullets, bombs or the weapons of this world. They yield only to the Sword.

STORYTELLER: The Arms Dealer handed Kai'Ro a small, but very sharp Sword.

KAI'RO: Shoot, this thing is tiny! You sure I can do some damage with this?

ARMS DEALER: Don't you worry 'bout the size of the blade in your hand, friend. This here Sword is not made for tearin' stuff up. It's the weapon of a skilled warrior that is thrust forward only once to deal a deadly blow. It's an assassin's blade. Yer other weapons are made to protect yer heart and soul from destruction.

STORYTELLER: The Arms Dealer placed a Helmet on Kai'Ro's head, a Breastplate on his chest and some crazy looking Shoes on his feet. Then he handed him a light Shield.

KAI'RO: I feel kinda foolish wearin' this stuff. I mean, nobody wears this kinda stuff.

ARMS DEALER: The King's Armor has stood out since the beginnin' of time. There's nothin' like it and anyone who sees it knows that the one who wears it and uses it belongs to the King. But the Armor ain't heavy and clunky. It's light so you can move quickly, but it's strong to keep you safe.

STORYTELLER: Kai'Ro looked himself over, as if he was trying to figure out how he felt about everything.

KAI'RO: So, why's all the Armor have 116 on it?

ARMS DEALER: It's a reminder from the King's Word. It reminds the wearer of the Armor that there ain't no shame in the Gospel. Any man or woman who wears this Armor must go into battle and into every town unashamed. You must also be willin' to face any friend or foe with the power of the Gospel.

KAI'RO: I can feel that.

ARMS DEALER: You are now an ambassador for the King. Yer an agent of reconciliation to a dyin' world. Yer equipped to do battle with the powers of hell. You now have heavenly weapons that can destroy strongholds. When you must fight, do everything you can to stand.

As a good soldier, don't get yerself tangled up in the treasure and traps of this world. Use the Shield of the Faith to protect yerself 'gainst the blows of the enemy when he strikes to crush you. Let the Helmet of Salvation remind you always that yer saved and that you belong to the King. The Breastplate of Righteousness will guard yer heart and keep it secure. The Shoes on yer feet are the Shoes of Peace.

Sometimes you'll face enemies that ain't gonna back down to the Sword, 'n so you must keep goin' forward in prayer. Pray for yerself, pray for the King's Kingdom to go forth, and pray for all of yer fellow soldiers. You hear what I'm sayin'?

KAI'RO: Yeah, I feel you.

ARMS DEALER: Remember that this battle is 24/7. There ain't *no breaks* from this fight. Don't fall back and don't get lazy. Some folks will tuck and run when the heat gets turned up. Some will get bored, others captured, 'n a few may even become traitors like that boy, Demas. Stand yer ground and the King will always provide you with what you need. Those who fight the good fight are more than conquerors. Even their enemies become their slaves.

The Armor is yours to wear day and night. Never take it off or forget about it—or you may get thrashed. It will guard you and keep you effective in our struggle for the King's Kingdom.

I gotta tell you that you'll prob'ly suffer, you'll hurt, 'n you may even die in this battle here. But, rejoice that you can bear the wounds 'n scars of yer King, for your reward is great in His Kingdom. The harder you fight, the more yer soul will blaze with fire. And the more yer joy will grow. There is no greater callin' or greater boost to your soul than to live and die as a soldier! You will have all of eternity to enjoy a break from the battle.

KAI'RO: By the King's grace, I will stand. Everything you have said makes my heart burn inside me. I'm still pretty new to this whole thing. Pray for me.

ARMS DEALER: Well, it's time for you to go. I will pray fer ya. As with all good soldiers, I will see you on the other side of the River. Now go start fightin' the good fight. It ends with your death.

DOIN' BATTLE 9

STORYTELLER: Kai'Ro left the Arms Dealer wearing his new Armor. He appeared a little awkward in it at first. But the more he walked, the more comfortable he looked. A few people stopped from time to time to watch him as he passed by them on the path. Some pointed and snickered, some looked confused, and a few others just stared in amazement.

After a while, Kai'Ro came into an open field. From the other side, he saw a man approaching him in a nice dark suit. The Man stopped him as they drew close. The suit he had on looked very expensive. He had diamonds in his ears and a dark chain with a snake on it around his neck. There was a strange look in his eyes.

MAN: Where are you coming from?

KAI'RO: I'm from the City of Doom.

MAN: And where are you going?

KAI'RO: I'm on my way to the City of Light.

MAN: So you're leaving the City of Doom? Why would you ever do that?

KAI'RO: Because that place is goin' to be judged by the King. It's an evil place full of evil people. I used to be a part of all that.

But then I found out through Preacher that if I stayed there, I was goin' to be judged right along with the city.

MAN: Judged! That's crazy talk! For one, the City of Doom is a place of peace, pleasure and prosperity. This road you're on now is loaded with pain and loneliness. I'll bet that ol' fool left that part out.

KAI'RO: Depends on what you mean by pain. Yeah, I know that traveling on this Heavenly Highway is hard and painful. But it isn't nearly as painful as the burden of my sinful conscience or the fear I had in my soul about dyin' without knowin' the King. When you talk about peace and pleasure in the City of Doom...it's not for real. I mean, that stuff is cool for a while—but it don't satisfy your soul. It's an awful and stinkin' place and I haven't had no regrets.

MAN: What is so awful about pleasure? Is it so wrong to get for your-self things that make you feel good? Things that make you powerful? It sounds like this King is keeping you from a lot of stuff that could make your life a whole lot better. What kind of King is *that*?

KAI'RO: That's one spin you can put on it. But like I said to you, that stuff just don't satisfy. It's like bein' real thirsty and tryin' to drink out of a cup with a buncha holes in it. I mean, you can get a little in your mouth, but most of it just falls on the ground and leaves you thirsty. My whole life was like that cup for the longest. I kept puttin' stuff in it, but most of it just went right through me without satisfyin' my thirst.

Besides that, most of the stuff that I was puttin' in my body and puttin' in my soul was poison. It was doin' some seri-ous damage on me. Too much smokin', drinkin', hustlin' and all that stuff is sheer poison, dawg. Sin is what it is, and it leads a brotha to death.

If you wanna talk about pleasure, real pleasure is found in the King and in Him gettin' the glory. It's also found in walkin'

His path of Life. On that path He gives me joy and pleasures, for real. His pleasures ain't necessarily money and fame, but they're peace, hope and security. I've found pleasure and purpose on this road that I'm on now. That stuff back in the City of Doom wasn't no lastin' kinda pleasure.

MAN: So you left all of that in exchange for some promise of the King? What exactly is *He* giving to you that's so good? I can tell you right now that there's nothing down this road that will lead to happiness. This is a road of tears and frustration...

KAI'RO: Maybe, but who ever said that this life's 'bout happiness anyway? What I got now is joy. I found joy at the Cross when my burden rolled away. I found out that I wasn't guilty no more and that I was no longer an enemy of the King. Happiness comes and goes. I used to be happy when I came home with a stack of dough from hustlin'. But as soon as it was gone, my happiness went with it. It was the same with the girls and parties. That stuff just didn't stay.

But joy, dawg, joy is buried deep down in my soul—and no one can take that from me. I know that the King loves me and there's nothin' that can separate me from that love. No *man* can separate me, no *demons,* and not even *death* can separate me from the love the King's got for me. That's pure *joy,* dawg.

STORYTELLER: As Kai'Ro continued to talk, the Man fell back a little. Then, to my surprise, he started to transform altogether. His skin grew shiny and scaly like the flesh of a snake. His suit started to rip apart as two large black wings burst from his back. Then he began to grow in size. Two red horns like the horns of a ram grew out of the sides of his head, and fire and smoke emerged from his mouth. Long, sharp claws grew from his fingers like the talons of an eagle. He reared one of his hands back and took a swipe at Kai'Ro. But just as he did so, Kai'Ro spun around and raised his Shield.

KAI'RO: How long did you think you could fool me with your smooth talk, Diablo? I know you're the prince of demons. You were tryin' to drag my heart back to my old ways, and you were tryin' to fill me with despair 'bout where I'm goin'. I *recognized* your lies!

DIABLO: I have been waiting for you to come down this road and now you're all *mine!*

KAI'RO: I can tell you right now, you best get outta my way. Or I'll send you home hoppin'.

DIABLO: Who are you to talk to *me,* you filthy human?

KAI'RO: I ain't no filthy human. I belong to King of Kings and I am one of His sons. I'm made in the image of the King. I know who you are, you son of the devil, and I don't belong to you no more!

DIABLO: No, you are a son of my city, the City of Doom. You belong to *me,* you hopeless, wretched fool. If you turn around to where you came from, I will show you my mercy and spare your life.

KAI'RO: I can never go back! I'm in this thing, for real. I'm no fool. I was one once, but now my Father is a King, and I share in His righteousness. The King has purchased me from your stinkin' hands!

DIABLO: You have left the City of Doom, a place of pleasure and pride, for a life of hardship and pain. No good King would set you on such a path. If you stay on this path, you are the stupidest man I have ever met! If you return, I will lavish upon you wealth, fame and power. My ways were not harsh and my City was a place where you were great, O Kai'Ro of the City of Doom!

KAI'RO: That is no longer my name, you lyin' snake! I'm Kai'Ro, the son of the King. My new home is in the City of Light. It is true when you say that your ways were not harsh, and it is true that I was a great man in my old town. But I was under the Law, I was under wrath, and I was locked up in your doggone chains. You had plans to drag my soul with you to hell!

Besides, all those things you promised me if I go back...they ain't yours anyway. Everything in this world be-longs to the King—even you! Don't front like you got anything to offer me. You got nothin' to offer, for real. In fact, you're flat broke, dawg! You're just a puppet on strings.

Now, know this. I'm not goin' back. I will not give you my soul. The wealth and power that you're tryin' to pawn off on me is trash in comparison to what my King's got waitin' for me in His Kingdom. Now...step off!

DIABLO: Where are you going to go, foolish one? Do you really think this King will accept you? *You*, a drug dealer, a man of violence, and a man who could go through women like a kid through a bag of candy? You have stolen from your own mother, cursed your neighbors, and lied to your pastor. You are an embarrassment. You have already failed multiple times on this journey of yours. Like an idiot, you fell into the Swamp of Despair. You lost your Scroll just moments after you went to the loathsome Cross. At the Keeper's house, you had lustful thoughts about his virgin daughters.

You are a sick, despicable impostor, Kai'Ro. Do you think this King of yours will allow someone as ugly and wretched as you into His house? Come back to me, for you are like all of my children. I will let you do as you wish.

KAI'RO: All that you've said is true, but you forget that the King took all my stink and sin with Him on the Cross. I'm clean as can be. He took all my sins and gave me His righteousness. You got *nothin'* on me! There is no condemnation for those who belong to the King.

Back with you, I stood judged with every breath I took. I was on a speedin' highway straight to the pit of hell. Naw! You best be goin' because I'll never place myself under you again. I will die before I go back to that life again.

DIABLO: Then you will get your wish, fool. I will thrash and throttle the very life out of you! Then I'll drag your carcass back for your old friends to consider. They'll be rid of your foolish ideas forever.

KAI'RO: You're the fool, playa! You really don't get it, do you? You kill me and then you send me to Life, for real. For me, to live in this life is to live for the King! But to die? Man, to die is gain, dawg! You'll give me a one-way ticket to the City of Light and that's cool with me. I can't wait to see my King face-to-face. Either way, you're goin' to be in for a brutal fight before you take this brotha down!

STORYTELLER: Diablo suddenly fired a hail of blazing darts at Kai'Ro. They came at him as thick as a cloud of angry hornets. Kai'Ro lifted up his Shield and the darts thudded against it like stones bouncing off of a tin roof. Only a few of them struck him in the foot, the shoulder and the head. Kai'Ro stood his ground, but the fiery darts just kept coming and coming.

Soon he started to get tired. His Sword was pulled out, but Diablo stayed far enough away that he couldn't be reached. More darts continued to hit Kai'Ro until one snuck through and struck him right in the chest. He stumbled backwards.

The battle lasted for hours as the prince demon fired dart after dart at Kai'Ro. I could see that the young warrior was growing wearier with each moment. For a split second, it looked like he was going to turn and run. But then the 116 on his shield caught his eye and he remembered what the Arms Dealer had told him. He stood his ground.

KAI'RO: (to himself) If I turn and run from this cat, he'll light me up in the back and I'll fall for sure. Plus, if I resist the enemy, I'm sure he'll be the one who'll do the runnin' in the end.

STORYTELLER: I could tell that Diablo was getting frustrated with Kai'Ro's courage. So he decided to try another tactic, this time making things more personal. He spread his wings apart and, from behind his back, he pulled out a flaming sword and a fiery ball and chain. On the hilt of the sword was the word SHAME and on the ball and chain was the word DISCOURAGE-MENT.

These were potent weapons. He charged at Kai'Ro hard and swung the ball and chain at him. The fiery ball crashed against Kai'Ro's shield like a blast of thunder. Kai'Ro's entire body shook. Then the powerful demon came at him with his sword. Kai'Ro was able to knock back his first strike, but the second one got behind his Shield and gave him a huge wound in his side. Kai'Ro let out a yell and dropped his Sword. Diablo's red eyes flashed brightly and he swung his ball and chain one more time.

This time Kai'Ro was able to raise up his Shield a little, but the ball bounced off his Shield and almost knocked his Helmet off. The wounded warrior fell to the ground and gritted his teeth in pain. Almost all of the hope faded out of his eyes.

Diablo moved in for the kill. He stepped over Kai'Ro and grabbed him by his throat.

DIABLO: I told you that you belong to *me*. You became mine the day you were born, you stupid fool. I gave you a chance to give up, turn around, and go back to business as usual. Now you're just damaged goods and I have no use for you anymore. I'm going to spill your blood and snatch the life out of you!

STORYTELLER: Diablo raised his sword above him to deliver a final, crushing blow. But as he did so, Kai'Ro reached out his arm as far as it would stretch and snatched up his Sword that had fallen on the ground. Without hesitating, he drove the blade deep into Diablo's stomach and screamed a great shout of victory!

KAI'RO: Rejoice not over me, O my enemy. When I fall, I shall rise . . .

STORYTELLER: Diablo groaned in pain and a long trail of bright red fire burst from his mouth and eyes. He spread his great wings and took off into the air, cursing and howling until he disappeared over some hills. Kai'Ro gasped and let out a deep breath of relief. With great pain, he rolled over onto his bloodied hands and knees. He was badly hurt and could hardly stand, yet somehow he managed to pull himself to his feet. Limping over to a rock, he sat down to rest for a moment.

KAI'RO: (in prayer) Thank you, Father, for savin' my life from the devil. I rejoice that You who are in me is greater than he who is in the world. Please give me the strength to keep goin'. I'm hurt bad.

STORYTELLER: Wincing in pain, Kai'Ro slowly pulled out his old Bible and read some words of encouragement. As he read, he began to feel a bit stronger. He drank some water and ate some food that the Keeper had given him. Then he returned to his Bible and read, "Let us then with confidence draw near to the throne of grace, that we may receive mercy and find grace to help in time of need."

Kai'Ro smiled and closed his eyes.

THE ALLEY OF THE SHADOW OF DEATH

10

STORYTELLER: Soon Kai'Ro was able to get himself together, and he started down the Heavenly Highway again. His Armor had taken a real beating, but it had saved his life. He walked on for a while down the Highway until it appeared to dip down into a long, dark Alley.

Stopping for a moment, he took a hard look. The Alley was full of thick smog and I could hear strange and evil noises rumbling from the deep. Kai'Ro swallowed hard. Just then, a man came running towards him from out of the Alley. He had on Armor like Kai'Ro's but was missing his Sword. The poor man's Helmet was about to fall off.

KAI'RO: Yo, man, where you goin'?

DESERTER: Man, don't even think about goin' down there, dawg! I barely made it out of there with my life. That place is as scary as it can be! I ain't lyin'.

KAI'RO: Yeah, you ain't lyin'. It looks real scary to me too. That doesn't mean I'm not gonna go down there.

DESERTER: It was some stuff down there that I've never seen before, homie. I mean, some crazy monsters, goblins, ghosts...all kinda things. Plus, a Cloud of Confusion is all around you, and you can't see nothin'. The whole place is full of Death, man. I split outta there so fast. There was no way I was gonna try to make it through there.

KAI'RO: Maybe if we go together we can keep each other safe. Two is better than one, right?

DESERTER: Naw, dawg. This is as far as I'm gonna go.

KAI'RO: There's no goin' back for a true soldier of the King. You should know that! Get yourself together, man, 'cause you can't go back now.

DESERTER: Man, later for this! I told you I ain't goin' down there again. If you got any brains, you won't do it either, homie.

STORYTELLER: Kai'Ro frowned as Deserter ran off. He turned to face the dark Alley before him. Tightening the chin strap on his Helmet, he pulled out his Sword and started walking. As he descended into the mouth of the Alley, it grew darker and darker. Before long, the sun itself appeared to vanish until there was hardly any light at all. The air was hot and thick with smoke and strange shadows seemed to race back and forth across the main road. He found himself walking on a long stretch of cracked concrete.

Things were strangely quiet, like a town from a zombie movie. On either side of the road were thick, grey brick walls that rose up so high that no one could climb them. In certain parts of the walls were large holes and cracks. If anyone was to make it through this Alley, they would have to go straight through it.

Up ahead was a metal garbage can with burning trash inside. Two cloaked creatures glared at Kai'Ro as he drew near. Strange orange eyes burned inside their cloaks. When they slashed at Kai'Ro and hissed, I could see that their sharp, talon-like fingers resembled bird claws. Kai'Ro held up his Sword at them and they slunk back.

Occasionally, a street lamp would flicker on and off. At one point, one of the lights flashed and I saw a faded green street sign that read BAD MEMORIES BOULEVARD. The road narrowed quite a bit as Kai'Ro continued to walk. Some strange red lights along the walls were the only things that gave Kai'Ro an idea where to go.

Up ahead, I saw a young man in a black T-shirt mercilessly kicking and beating another young man who was rolling around on the ground, begging for help. Kai'Ro saw that the man on the ground didn't have much fight left, so he ran up to help.

KAI'RO: Hey, dawg, what'cha doin'? Lay off! You hear me? Lay off that dude!

STORYTELLER: As soon as Kai'Ro raced up to the young man who was laying out the beating, he put his hand on his shoulder to stop him. The young man in the black T-shirt spun around. Kai'Ro jumped back in total shock. The face staring back at him was his own. The other Kai'Ro burst into laughter and took off running into the shadows. When Kai'Ro was able to regain his senses, he stooped down to help the young man on the ground. The guy was bleeding badly out of his nose, mouth and ears.

KAI'RO: Hey, man, it's all right now. He's gone. You're gonna be all right.

STORYTELLER: The man on the ground started hollering at Kai'Ro and trying to squirm out of his grasp.

MAN: Naw, get away from me! Why won't you leave me alone? What'd I ever do to you?

STORYTELLER: Kai'Ro looked down at the man and tried to help him again. Then, the man suddenly disappeared like a puff of smoke.

KAI'RO: (sadly to himself) I remember that poor dude. I put that cat in the hospital for like two weeks, all because I thought he was the one talkin' to my girl. Man, I messed that guy up for nothin'. Can't believe I did that...

STORYTELLER: Unsure of what to do, Kai'Ro decided to keep going forward. He was bothered. He went on a ways further until he spotted a young man in a bright red shirt rummaging hurriedly through a big black purse. The young man looked up every now and then, as if he was on the lookout for someone. Just beyond this young man, I spotted a little boy in the shadows watching the man going through the purse.

Kai'Ro came up closer to the thief. But as soon as he got within a few feet, the other young man turned to face him. Just like earlier, the face of the one staring back at him was his own. The young thief smiled a big smile at Kai'Ro, burst into laughter and then took off running. As he did so, Kai'Ro saw the little boy in the shadows and a look of total embarrassment covered his face.

KAI'RO: Ah, naw... not my lil' brotha! Come here, Lil' One! Come here. Your big bro ain't like that no more. I don't steal from Moms no more. C'mon, Lil' One. Don't run off, shortie! Come back here!

STORYTELLER: Lil' One just burst into tears, shook his head at Kai'Ro and then ran off deep into the shadows. But then, just down the way, another Kai'Ro look-alike was leaning on the wall. This one was smoking a joint. Just beyond him was his brother, Lil' One, watching through a window in one of the walls. Then another Kai'Ro appeared wearing a backpack. He was walking with two friends and talking.

KAI'RO LOOK-ALIKE: This is the last day I'm goin' to school, dawg. How much have we learned in the last two years? Man, we ain't learned nothin'! I was talkin' to Dealer just yesterday and he said he could hook all of us up if we wanted to start hustlin'. I told him I was down, what about ya'll?

STORYTELLER: I watched this Kai'Ro take his backpack full of school books and sling it into a dumpster. The two boys who were with him did the same thing. Lil' One was walking a few feet behind them. He was listening the whole time. He stopped at the dumpster and looked at it for a minute. Then the young boy stared as he watched his brother walk off into the distance. Lil' One took off his own backpack, tossed it into the dumpster and then took off in a different direction. At this point, the real Kai'Ro had seen enough. He folded both of his hands over his face and started to cry.

KAI'RO: O God, don't let this be for real! I'm so sorry 'bout all that stuff. I pray that my little brotha didn't see me do all that terrible stuff. Don't let Lil' One go down the same road as me, please. I'm beggin' you, God! Please don't let him make the same mistakes as me. Please! I'm cryin' out to You to restore the locust years to my little brotha. Please make right whatever I made wrong by my own mistakes. Only You can fix this, for real. I messed up so bad, but I know You can make anything right again if You're willin'.

STORYTELLER: As he continued on, there were more Kai'Ro look-alikes appearing before him for almost as far as the eye could see. They were fighting, cursing, stealing and wandering around with scandalous-looking girls. Feeling somewhat discouraged, Kai'Ro started to turn around. But as he did so, a small glimmer of light flashed on the outside of his shield, showing him the 116. He let out a deep sigh and looked up towards Heaven, even though there was no way he could see it from the Alley.

KAI'RO: (to himself) If anyone is the King's son, he is a new creation. The old has passed away; behold, the new has come. Thank you, my King. I don't have to live in my past, as ugly as it is. I can forget what's behind me and press on towards what's before me. By your grace, I'll go on.

STORYTELLER: As Kai'Ro prayed, the Alley cleared and he was able to walk for a while without any more bad memories emerging before him. Finally, BAD MEMORIES BOULEVARD ended. Within a short distance, he came to STRANGLE-HOPE STREET. This Street was narrow and even darker than the Boulevard he had just left. There were horrible noises bouncing off the walls and coming towards Kai'Ro. There were groans, shrieks and loud roars. Kai'Ro swallowed hard and hesitated for the moment. Then he pulled his Shield closer to his body and raised his Sword.

KAI'RO: (to himself) If the King is for me . . . who can be against me?

STORYTELLER: He plunged forward into the street. The further he went, the narrower the street became. It wasn't long before he almost had to turn sideways just to fit. The metal of his Shield and Breastplate actually scraped up against the walls, and he was forced to move slowly.

Just then, a slimy arm from out of a hole in the wall grabbed him around the throat. Kai'Ro yelled and struggled until he was able to free himself. He hadn't gone far before something white and ugly like a ghost came down upon him and tried to push him through a hole in the wall. Kai'Ro flailed at the spirit with his Sword until it released him.

Behind the walls there was a horrible roaring sound and loud thuds as if a huge creature on the other side was trying to break through and devour him. Sometimes sudden explosions of fire would shoot out from the walls and blast against Kai'Ro's Shield, pinning him against the wall behind him. This terrible Street went on for miles and Kai'Ro was only able to go at a slow pace because there was hardly any room to move.

Then I saw a skinny spirit sneak up behind him. The unclean spirit was shriveled and decayed like a corpse. It came up close to Kai'Ro until the disgusting face was right on his shoulder. It started to whisper spiteful things into his ears. It whispered horrible things about the King and about His Kingdom. For a moment, it was obvious that Kai'Ro was ashamed because he believed that these thoughts were his own. Then I heard him cry out.

KAI'RO: Naw! I gotta take every thought captive. Get off me, you foul demon! Get ya poison outta my head! Those thoughts ain't my thoughts. That's nothin' but poison!

STORYTELLER: The ugly spirit disappeared into the darkness. But instantly, three little red goblins scurried down the walls and climbed on top of Kai'Ro. One of them had a little hammer with the word IRRITATION on it. He started beating Kai'Ro in the face and on the head. Kai'Ro tried to knock it off, but the goblin was too quick and would dodge his blows and then smack him again from a different angle.

One of the other goblins snuck down to his legs and started sticking him with a sharp pin called WEARINESS. The more he stuck him, the slower Kai'Ro moved. He swatted at this goblin but, like the first one, he was too quick and avoided all of Kai'Ro's blows.

The third goblin had a syringe full of a liquid called FEAR. He jabbed it into Kai'Ro's neck just below his Helmet. At this point, Kai'Ro stumbled to his knees and his Sword fell from his limp hands.

KAI'RO: I can't go no further in this evil place.

STORYTELLER: I could tell he was becoming more and more discouraged. But with what strength he had left, he picked up his Sword and struggled to his feet. Slowly, with a lot of effort, he was able to turn his body around. The goblins started laughing and hitting and sticking him even more. But just then, a voice came echoing down the Alley walls. It was a welcome voice, as the man was reciting the 23rd Psalm: "Tho I walk thru the Alley of the Shadow of Death, I will fear no evil, for You are with me. Your rod and Your staff, they comfort me."

Kai'Ro quickly spun back the other way again with a look of joy on his face. With renewed strength, he hollered out.

KAI'RO: Hey, dawg, don't leave me! Lemme catch up to you! Wait up!

STORYTELLER: His voice bounced off a ways down the walls, but there was no response. Still Kai'Ro was encouraged and started moving forward again with more speed and determination than he had before.

The goblins continued hitting and sticking him, but he didn't appear to notice anymore. After a while, they snarled and gave up. Scurrying back up the walls again, they looked like rats racing up a drainpipe. Still, there were slimy and scaly arms that grabbed at Kai'Ro through the walls.

At one point, he could hardly move because there were so many hands grabbing, pushing and pulling at him. Some tried to snatch off his Helmet and others struggled to rip his Shield out of his hands. Kai'Ro slashed and lashed with his Sword and tried to beat them back so that he could continue going. He gritted his teeth.

KAI'RO: (encouraging himself) I will fear no evil in this Alley. Even here...the King is with me...there's nowhere for me to go where He ain't already there, watchin' me. I gotta press on. I gotta keep goin'!

STORYTELLER: The strange creatures in the walls grew even more aggressive. A few actually crawled out of their holes like worms out of the ground. They had razor-edged teeth and pointed red eyes. They hissed and spat and tried to slash at Kai'Ro with their claws or sink their fangs into his flesh. His Sword and Shield were excellent weapons in this place and he was able to beat most of his attackers back into their holes. Even so, every now and then, he would get scratched or bitten and would yell out in pain.

Then all of a sudden, he shook free from the hostile monsters like one falling through a wall of thick branches. He fell into an open space again where he was able to stand and move about with more freedom. When he stood up, there before him was something that nearly caused him to fall out. It was a large black hole with a narrow cement bridge running across the middle of it. The bridge itself had a slick green moss growing on top of it. Just before the bridge was an old crumbled sign with graffiti on it that read: "The blind lead the blind."

Kai'Ro eased up to the edge of the pit and looked down. It was full of bones and bodies. There was a foul smell coming up from out of it. It was dark, but I could see that some of the bodies were still moving a little. They were groaning and crying for help but were far too deep in the pit for any person to pull them out.

KAI'RO: Man, I don't know about this. It reminds me of the pit that David fell into a long time ago. I've come so far through this horrible place, but that bridge is so doggone slick. If I fall off one way or the other I'm really done for. I wanna go back, but maybe I'm almost outta here.

STORYTELLER: As he waited at the edge of the bridge in deep thought, I saw another man already walking a ways down from where Kai'Ro was standing. Kai'Ro looked up and spotted him too. The other man was walking quickly but carefully so that he wouldn't slip.

KAI'RO: If that cat can make it, then so can I. That's gotta be that same dude from earlier. Maybe if I can catch up to him we can hang out and do this whole thing together.

STORYTELLER: With as much courage as he could muster, Kai'Ro stepped out onto the bridge. It was slipperier than he thought. And he almost lost his footing and fell into the pit after his first step. As he was flailing his arms and trying to regain his balance, he looked down and saw a decaying body covered and surrounded by a bunch of CDs that Kai'Ro used to listen to.

KAI'RO: Man, I remember listenin' to all that stuff. Those CDs were like my Bible back then. What those guys said to me was the truth. Back then those rappers were the truth to me. Hip-hop used to be my father, but now the King is my Daddy.

STORYTELLER: He regained his balance and started walking again. This time, he was more careful with each step, but the bridge itself started to zigzag back and forth. Everything around him grew darker and darker until he couldn't even see the next step in front of him. He was forced to stop because he knew that his next step could be his last.

KAI'RO: What do I do now? It's so dark that I can't go forward or backwards 'cause I'll fall for sure.

STORYTELLER: Kai'Ro stood there hopelessly perplexed for a minute. Like anyone who is lost and confused, he started to panic. But then a small light appeared around him. It was just a faint glow, but it caught his eyes and he looked down.

KAI'RO: (with a sudden burst of confidence) Aw, c'mon, Kai'Ro, you're smarter than this! You got a way outta this mess wit you right now.

STORYTELLER: Kai'Ro reached into his back pocket and pulled out his Bible. As he opened it, a shaft of light shot out and gave him just enough light to see the next step in front of him. Kai'Ro's entire face lit up with joy and he began to speak words from his Bible.

KAI'RO: Your Word is a lamp to my feet and a light to my path! No wonder so many folks have fallen off this road...without this Word, they're walkin' this dark road in total blindness!

STORYTELLER: He kept his Word open for the rest of the time on the bridge. The road remained slick, and even though he was still frightened by the horrible stuff in the pit below, he was able to make it to the other side. Just as he crossed over, a thin beam of sunlight started to push through the darkness and the fog. I could see that the Alley actually started to ascend up onto level ground again. Kai'Ro started moving quickly, anxious to leave that horrible Alley behind him.

The further he climbed out, the brighter it became. At one point, he stopped and looked behind him. From his higher position, he could see most of the Alley laid bare. He saw the thin bridge crossing the pit and he saw the terrible STRANGLE-HOPE STREET with all the monsters and goblins. As the light pushed farther onto the Alley, all of the evil things shrieked and ducked into the holes in the walls. It was a holy light that shone down on the Alley and all the evil below gave way to it. Kai'Ro turned around again with a big smile on his face.

Just up ahead he noticed another man like himself. The young man had on the same Armor covering some baggy jeans and a white-T. From this distance, Kai'Ro recognized the man and yelled to him.

KAI'RO: Phanatik! It's me, Kai'Ro, dawg! Wait up!

CATCHIN' UP

11

STORYTELLER: Phanatik pressed on, refusing to turn around. It was obvious that he was in a hurry to get away from the Alley too.

Kai'Ro decided to sprint to catch up and soon began closing in on him. Starting to gain some momentum, he picked up his pace but then raced right by Phanatik. When he tried to slow down, Kai'Ro tripped and fell down hard. He laid there for a minute until Phanatik caught up to him and helped him to his feet.

KAI'RO: Thanks, homie.

STORYTELLER: Kai'Ro felt embarrassed as Phanatik pulled him up. But I could tell he was overjoyed to see a fellow traveler.

KAI'RO: Man, Phanatik! I can't believe it's really you, dawg!

PHANATIK: Yeah, frat. I heard you headed off down this Highway.

KAI'RO: I had no idea you were on this road too, man. But then the Keeper told me that you had passed through.

PHANATIK: Yeah, when I heard you had left the City of Doom and took off on this trip, I was like "Man, I gotta catch up so we can do this thing together." You left just before I could get ahold of you.

STORYTELLER: The two brave travelers started walking side by side down the road, anxious to talk about their journeys so far.

KAI'RO: Man, I had no idea you were feelin' this whole thing. I had no clue that you were thinkin' about comin' along.

PHANATIK: Yeah, Preacher caught up with me 'bout the same time he got with you. I had been goin' through some stuff in my life around that time and was really lookin' for some hope. Until I met him, I was givin' my all to the thug life, ya know? I mean, I was into the hustlin' real deep and I was makin' more money than a man knows what to do with. You knew what I was up to, dawg, you saw how I was livin'.

KAI'RO: Yeah, you were livin' large. Everybody knew your name.

PHANATIK: It just wasn't sittin' right with me. I had everything goin' for me, but inside I was just feelin' terrible. It wasn't really that long before I ran into Preacher. I was chillin' one day in one of my Benzs and he just rolled up on me. I thought he was trippin' and even reached for my piece the way he came up on me. But when he opened his mouth and started talkin' about my life and how miserable I was, I just couldn't do nothin' but listen to what he was sayin'. Somehow he just knew about all the drama that was goin' on inside my head.

Then when he started talkin' 'bout this Heavenly Highway and that there was a way to get right with God, I was like "Man, what this cat is sayin' is dope, for real." He told me I'd have to put the hustlin' aside forever if I was goin' to do this thing. When he said that, I started feelin' this burden on my back. But I was thinkin' there was no way I could do that. I mean, how could I give up the lifestyle I had goin' on with the girls, the cash and the pleasure? I felt all torn up inside.

I guess it's when I heard that you had taken off on the same journey that I decided I could prob'ly do it too. I mean, you and I were never really friends, but you were the one guy who had my respect...

KAI'RO: That's tight, dawg. My story is pretty much the same.

STORYTELLER: Kai'Ro told Phanatik about the first stage of his journey when he and Quitter and Follower stopped off at the House of Mockers. He mentioned how they fell into the Swamp of Discouragement and then how Quitter and Follower left him high and dry.

PHANATIK: Yeah, those two cats came runnin' back to the City of Doom like two scared puppies. They was all covered in mud and stuff and it was like they was tryin' to duck and dodge back to their houses. But everybody knew they had gone wit you. Then when they came back, they tried so hard to play the whole thing off.

Nobody was buyin' it, though. Everyone started crackin' on those guys so bad for how they whimped out like that. Man, it wouldn't let up. Those two fools were so humiliated that they hardly came out of the house no more. It woulda been better for them if they had drowned in that Swamp because they came back lookin' like a coupla scared clowns.

KAI'RO: Yeah, it's like they just dropped outta the race. It's better to never start racin' or fightin' if you ain't gonna finish what you started. So, I 'spose you ran into Worldly Wiseman?

PHANATIK: Naw. I never saw that dude. After hearin' all about your little adventure in the Swamp, I was able to find the foot path and keep myself from fallin' in. After I got down the path a ways, it started to get dark. I was lookin' for a place to crash and that's when I ran into a beautiful girl named Bliss. This girl was *too* fine. She had a little house just 'round the way. And when I was goin' by, she was standin' there in the doorway like she was watchin' for me or somethin'. She had on these lil' shorts and a tight shirt that was leavin' nothin' up to the imagination.

That girl had one of those looks on her face that can draw a brotha in. She called out to me as I was walkin' by. She said,

"Hey, boy, come here. My man's gone off to town for business and he won't be back for 'bout two weeks. I've covered my bed with silk sheets and filled my room with some of the sweetest perfume a girl can buy. I've been to church and said my prayers, and now I'm ready for a little enjoyment. Why don't you come in here and spend some time with a lonely girl? I won't disappoint you." Dawg, I was tempted about as much as a brotha can be tempted.

KAI'RO: I hope you kept goin', 'cause that girl's house leads to death!

PHANATIK: Yeah, I know dude, but it took me and my thick head a minute or two to figure it out. I made a bad mistake. I got off the path and took a step towards her house. When I got up by her door, man, that girl grabbed me and kissed me like I've never been kissed before.

KAI'RO: What were you thinkin', dawg?

PHANATIK: That's the thing, I *wasn't* thinkin'. At least, I wasn't thinkin' with my heart. She pulled me into the bedroom and, just like she said, there were silk sheets on the bed. The room smelled better than anything I'd smelled before. She had some candles burnin' too. We were just 'bout to do our thing when I saw the blood.

KAI'RO: The blood?

PHANATIK: Yeah. There was a buncha sticky blood pooled up under the bed. It was a lotta blood, homie. I took one look at that blood, looked back at her, and then I dipped about as fast as a brotha' can run. She snatched at me and screamed at me to come back, but I was gone, dude.

KAI'RO: Man, girls like Bliss are a slaughter house, for real. You was like a lamb led to the slaughter. Girls like that can ruin a man, for real. How many guys do you and I know who've seen their lives end in a place like hers?

PHANATIK: Too many.

KAI'RO: You remember Lustful? He couldn't get enough girls. That poor fool got AIDs and died like two years ago. What about that cat named Playa? Man, that boy's got like three or four kids to support, and he can't even hardly hold down a job. Girls like Bliss? Shoot, there's a thousand ways they can kill a brotha.

PHANATIK: I know, frat. You tellin' it straight. It was the King's grace that got me outta there. Girls like Bliss have been a weakness for me as long as I can remember. I found out early on that just 'cause you start off on this Highway those temptations don't go away. It's been the King's good grace to me all along. After all those girls I been with in the past, I never got no disease and never got no girl pregnant.

I mean, that ain't just bein' lucky, dawg. That's just the King protectin' me from disaster. With Bliss, it was like the King gave me new eyes...take me back a few months, and there's no way I see the blood and the fact that she was a killa. I woulda been in some trouble, for real! Who knows what woulda happened to me?

KAI'RO: I'm glad you came to your senses, homie. When I ran into Worldly Wiseman, I almost made a bad decision too. He told me that I could lose my burden by headin' up to Legalopolis and gettin' a cat named Mac-Morality to remove the thing for me. I made a bad mistake and listened to him. Fortunately for me, Preacher caught up with me and set me straight.

PHANATIK: Yeah, praise the King for Preacher. The man found me just a short while after I ran from Bliss's house. He warned me that my flesh was still very much alive and that things might even get tougher the closer I got to the Cross. I appreciated him 'cause he was there for me. He could tell that I was real down, and he kinda jumped on me for bein' so stupid. But at the same time, he encouraged me and prayed for me. That did a lot to keep me goin'.

STORYTELLER: The two continued to walk and talk. They both shared stories about some of the different travelers they ran into along the way. Both of them had similar experiences in Birdville and Rock City. Like Kai'Ro, Phanatik steered clear of Thornville, even though he said it was a strong temptation for him to check it out.

KAI'RO: What'd you think when the Arms Dealer first handed you that Armor?

PHANATIK: I ain't gonna lie. I didn't like it much at first 'cause it felt goofy and I knew it was goin' to stand out. I was already feelin' the pressure of just givin' my life to the King and promisin' to follow after Him. But this Armor made it clear, that if I was in this thing for real, I was really gonna stand out.

KAI'RO: Yeah, but it came in useful against Diablo, didn't it?

PHANATIK: Naw, I never saw him.

KAI'RO: Man, that prince-demon 'bout killed me! This Armor and the Sword saved my life.

PHANATIK: Well, I had to tussle with a few of the monsters in that awful Alley back there.

KAI'RO: That was a scary place, dawg.

PHANATIK: Scary, for real! It kinda came out of nowhere. I remember dippin' down a ways in the path and it was like I was just wanderin' through a ghost town or somethin,' but then the sun went down. As soon as the sun was gone, it was like somebody opened up the gates of hell. I mean, I had monsters comin' at me outta God only knows where. Those things were huge and scary and a few of them woulda killed me if it hadn't been for this Armor and Sword. I almost turned back at a few points because I couldn't see any hope in sight.

KAI'RO: Me neither. It was like hope got snuffed out down there. I felt like David when he said he found himself in a miry pit. I hope that place is behind us *forever*.

PHANATIK: Yeah, me too. But Preacher said that there'd be lots of different Alleys in this journey...dark places where our faith and hope would be put to the test. I hope that awful Alley back there was the worst of 'em.

KAI'RO: Maybe that experience will make us stronger next time. I hope we won't be so quick to feel like runnin'.

STORYTELLER: In my dream, I saw how much this time with Phanatik benefitted Kai'Ro. To find a friend who made the same powerful choice and was willing to walk it out was a huge encouragement to him. They talked and talked for a long time about what they both saw at Interpreter's house and other adventures from the trip. Then the subject turned to the Cross.

KAI'RO: You gotta tell me about how you felt when you got to the Cross, dawg!

PHANATIK: Aw, man, how do you describe *those* kinds of feelins'? I mean, I felt a whole buncha things. I felt like the total script of my life got flipped, for real. I felt things comin' and felt things goin'. Like I felt accepted, for real. I felt like I had a big Dad and that made me feel like I had a family. I never really had a pops 'cause my old man ran out on me right after I was born. But when I felt the King's grace and acceptance comin' on me, I felt so alive, dawg, just so alive!

KAI'RO: And what'd you feel headin' back?

PHANATIK: Shame. Guilt. Embarrassment. Fear of judgment. All that stuff just rolled down the hill into that open grave with my burden. It was like all the baggage I had been carryin' around in my soul just disappeared. I felt clean all over for the very first time in my life. What went tumblin' down that hill, man, was a buncha terrible things. I mean, a *buncha* terrible things I had done, frat. When the stain and guilt for all that stuff was washed away, I felt as free as a bird.

KAI'RO: You ain't lyin', homie. My rap sheet was over a mile long too. It felt unbelievable to know that the King took the blame for a guy like me. When Preacher first showed me how all my sins offended God and that I was eternally separated from Him because of my sin—I almost lost hope. I mean, when he told me that the debt of all my sins meant that I had to spend eternity in hell, I felt about as bad as a brotha can feel.

But then, when he told me that the King had paid my sin-debt on that Cross, I couldn't believe it. I mean, my sins were just too ugly...it was unbelievable love for Him to just step into my shoes and take the blame for me so that God and I could be in right relationship with each other. I mean, who'd *do* somethin' like that? There's a few cats who might take a bullet for a friend, but it's like He took a fatal bullet for the whole world...for folks who don't know Him, or even those who hate Him.

PHANATIK: Yeah, and to think that He was perfect. I mean, He never did anything wrong—not even once. And yet He was willin' to die for a dude as ugly as me, just so that I could have a right relationship with God...it's amazin', dawg! Simply amazin'.

REVEREND RELEVANT AND PASTOR PATHETIC

12

STORYTELLER: As the two continued to talk about the amazing sacrifice of the King on the Cross, I saw in my dream a gigantic church. It was made of bright red bricks and the steeple seemed to almost touch the clouds. There were massive stained glass windows and the grounds around the church were covered in beautiful flowers and bushes. Two men were standing on the bright white steps leading up to the church entrance, and they were having an intense discussion.

One of the men, the pastor of the church, was a middle-aged gentleman dressed in an expensive dark suit. He had a white silken kerchief sticking out of the pocket on his suit coat. There were shiny black shoes on his feet. The other man was dressed in an older brown suit that was rather plain and his shoes were a little shabby and worn. In his hand he was holding a small plastic bag full of canned goods. I perceived that the flashy-dressed man was named Pastor Pathetic and the man in the brown suit was Reverend Relevant.

In their journey along the Highway, Kai'Ro and Phanatik came upon the two men and the conversation they were having in front of the church.

PASTOR PATHETIC: Listen, I hear what you're saying. There's a lot of people in Struggle-Town that need food, shelter and all kinds of help. Those of us at Me-Myself-and-I Chapel would really love to help you guys down at In-His-Service but we can't do a whole lot right now.

REV. RELEVANT: I just don't get it, brother. How can you turn your back on all those needy people? I mean, who's going to tell them about the King? If it isn't our two churches, who's going to show them that the King is a good King who cares about their needs?

PASTOR PATHETIC: Look, you know about our new church. A lot of the folks in my congregation got tired of worshiping in Struggle-Town. You know, it's dirty there. The crime has gone up a lot in the past few years, and most of the people in my church stopped feeling safe down there.

So I got with my deacons and some of the leaders, and we decided we needed to worship further out where everybody felt better. That's why we built a multimillion dollar place right here on the edge of Happyville. Happyville's a nice town, brother. Now, with all of our money tied up in our new church, I can't go to my people and ask them to support your soup kitchen, or whatever it was you mentioned...

REV. RELEVANT: It's the School for the Lost Sheep...a school for fatherless boys and girls. It saddens me to see you guys just up and leave Struggle-Town like that. You and I grew up there. Your church was a real cornerstone in that community going all the way back to when your great-grandfather founded it. Now your old church is just a big, empty building. It's like another symbol of abandonment for the people there. Seems like so many churches are just tucking and running these days...

PASTOR PATHETIC: What do you mean, tucking and running? Is it a bad thing to get my people out of a no-good neighborhood and bring them some place safe where they don't have to worry about their cars getting busted into during the service?

We felt it was important to focus on taking our kids out of that garbage dump and giving them a real chance. That's why we have the Keep Our Kids Clean Multipurpose Center with three full-sized basketball courts. We built a state-of-the-art skating rink and our Crunk for the King Teen Sanctuary where they can have some amazing concerts and youth rallies. We got places now where our youth can stay out of trouble. You have to start thinking about the kids at some point, brother.

REV. RELEVANT: Yeah, but what about all the kids left walking the streets? Not every kid and every family has the means to get up and out of the hood like the families in your church. What about the kids who need positive role models? There's kids looking for good things to get involved with in the afternoon. Not everyone is gangbanging and not everyone is into the drug scene.

That's why I'm asking you to consider helping with our School for the Lost Sheep. We're offering some of the poor kids in Struggle-Town a chance for a real education, as well as an introduction to the King and His plans for them. Our goal is to give the youth in that area an opportunity to grow in a nurturing community and family environment instead of taking to the streets. In other words, our school is giving kids an alternative to the gangs and street life.

Diablo is peddling a lot of evil stuff to the people in Struggle-Town because there aren't too many other choices. He isn't offering any hope...he's offering violence, pain and addiction. We want our church to bring the King's hands and feet to the streets of Struggle-Town by providing the people with real hope. That's why we've kept our bodies there, and that's why In-His-Service isn't leaving. I'm just afraid that by moving out to Happyville, you and your church members aren't going to be making much of an impact anymore.

STORYTELLER: Pastor Pathetic started to frown. I could see that he was about to lose his temper.

PASTOR PATHETIC: Impact! I've got almost four thousand people coming to hear me preach every Sunday. Through satellite, almost another six thousand viewers tune in to hear what I've got to say. Our mass choir has sung all over the world. They've already recorded three platinum selling CDs. I have two best-selling books, *The Blessings of the King* and *O the Ways the King Seeks to Bless You, My Child*. My congregation brings in almost ten million dollars each year in tithes. Don't talk to me about impact, brother. Me-Myself-and-I is making an impact!

STORYTELLER: Kai'Ro and Phanatik had been listening quietly the whole time. Then Kai'Ro started getting a little irritated and stepped into the conversation.

KAI'RO: Excuse me. I know I'm kinda buttin' in on y'all, but this whole debate has got my attention. (turning to the well-dressed man) You said that your church tithes almost ten million dollars a year. I mean, that's phenomenal! About how much of that money makes it out to bless other people?

PASTOR PATHETIC: (laughing nervously) That's tough to say, son. Like I said to my brother here earlier, almost everything right now is going to the bank to pay for our new church. We've got a roller-skating rink, basketball courts, and a church that can seat five thousand people. That's not cheap!

KAI'RO: With all due respect, it seems like Me-Myself-and-I is mainly concerned with *itself*. I mean, it seems from what I've read in the Word that the King wanted the church to be a tool for bringin' His Kingdom to a sin-strangled world. As I've read it, the King's people are supposed to bring hope to the hopeless, food to the hungry, clothing to the naked, and love to the hated. From everything I've heard you say, it sounds like you guys are doin' none of those things. In fact, I'd even say that your church is more worried about its own needs and good times and it doesn't even notice the needs just down the road.

PASTOR PATHETIC: Maybe you're hard of hearing, son. Did you not hear me say that I have over four thousand members in my church and another six thousand people who tune in through television? Most of those people were hopeless and hungry at one time. Now, I've got almost ten thousand people who've found hope and happiness. Do the math. My brother, Reverend Relevant, has a church of what? Two hundred and fifty? Who do you think the King is going to be happier with, ten thousand or two hundred and fifty?

KAI'RO: You're right. You've got a lot more people sittin' in your pews. But from the sound of things, that's all any of those people are ever goin' to do. *Sit.* I mean, my brother, Reverend Relevant, is tryin' to make disciples. From everything I've heard, he's tryin' to equip his people to get out on the streets and bring the King to the people through acts of service and ministry. They aren't just wastin' their lives.

Be honest. How's a skatin' rink gonna make disciples? Yeah, it'll give your people's kids somethin' to do on a Saturday night . . . maybe keep them out of trouble . . . but not much more beyond that. It sounds to me like you pulled up roots on the very community your great-granddaddy tried to help.

I thought the church was 'sposed to be salt and light. You know, it was called to help keep a community stable and to keep shooin' away the darkness by tellin' people about the Gospel and *showin'* them the Gospel. Seems like you and your church just snuffed your light right out. If you aren't meetin' the needs in the street and in the world around you, then you're just another building.

STORYTELLER: For a minute, Pastor Pathetic was stunned silent. He stared hard at Kai'Ro, as if he were thinking carefully about what to say next.

PASTOR PATHETIC: The King came to this earth, son, to make people happy. Without Him, the whole world is a real sad place.

My mission, and the mission of my church, is to make people happy in the King. We want people to hear how much the King loves them and how much He wants to make their lives better. There are thousands and thousands of people at my church who have heard that message and they've found that happiness. Our lives are happy. Our church is a happy place.

REV. RELEVANT: But that's just it, brother. Didn't the King say that the harvest is plentiful, but the workers are few? I agree that the King wants us to know that He loves us and wants to make our lives better. But then He wants us to take that message to anyone who hasn't heard or experienced His message yet. We're hardwired to go after what makes us happy. And if we aren't careful, we can keep that happy message and that happy focus all to ourselves. All the while, the rest of the world is being strangled by misery, addiction and hopelessness.

I think that the King wants us to find our joy in two things. One, He wants us to find our joy in Him. He wants us to discover that only a relationship with Him is what matters. Two, He wants us to find our joy in working with Him to bring a message of hope to a dying world. Seems like Me-Myself-and-I has found their joy in their own happiness, and until you understand part two, I have to agree with this young man here. Your church is just going to become another nice building on the other side of town.

I wish you would reconsider what I've asked you today. It would be a benefit to Struggle-Town for your people to give generously to some of the programs that I've mentioned. In fact, they could even volunteer to do some of the ministry work. It would also benefit your people because they'd experience joy like never before. Once they start joining the King in the work He's trying to do in our town, it would bring them a sense of true fulfillment.

PASTOR PATHETIC: I hear you. But like I said, our money is tied up in a huge mortgage note and in keeping our many programs going. We can't help you. And honestly, my people aren't *interested* in helping with that stuff anyway. It's time for me to be going. I have a sermon I need to prepare.

REV. RELEVANT: The greatest sermon you could ever preach is for your people to see you walking the streets of Struggle-Town again, bringing hope and new Life to your old community.

STORYTELLER: Without saying another word, Pastor Pathetic gave Kai'Ro, Phanatik and Reverend Relevant a passing wave and walked off quickly down the path.

KAI'RO: Sorry to crash your conversation like that. I just couldn't help but say somethin'.

REV. RELEVANT: (sighing) It's tough, son. It's getting harder and harder to persuade churches around here to step foot into gritty places. Some of them will cut a check from time to time. But to actually get laborers in this harvest down here, well, it's almost impossible.

KAI'RO: Well, I think churches like Me-Myself-and-I have lost their voice in the world. In fact, I think they're givin' the King a bad name. People look at all the drama and pain in the world, and then they see a lot of so-called followers of the King just locked away in their praise palaces down the road. It's like they don't even notice or care about all the hurt that's goin' on around them. The King lived a life of carin' and givin'. But when those who claim they're followin' Him don't do the same, man, it's just embarrassing.

STORYTELLER: Reverend Relevant held up the small sack of groceries in his hands.

REV. RELEVANT: Embarrassing is the right word, son. This little sack of groceries is all that Pastor Pathetic's church was able to provide for our ministry to twenty widows in our community. I got a chance to preach a night service there about six months ago. I bet two thousand people turned out. I preached about the King's love for orphans and widows and talked to them about our widow's ministry. I asked them to help with food and finances. One man cut me a check for fifty bucks, and this sack of groceries is all they provided in six months.

PHANATIK: That's ridiculous. Four thousand members and they can only buy three cans of baked beans and a coupla cans of tuna? That's sad!

KAI'RO: Yeah, but I bet they got some tight roller skates, homie!

STORYTELLER: All three burst into laughter.

KAI'RO: Look, I don't have a lot of money, but I appreciate what you're doin' in your town. Here's somethin' that will maybe help. Either way, I'm gonna keep you in my prayers. Thanks for inspirin' me and my man Phanatik here to keep bringin' the Gospel to the streets.

STORYTELLER: Kai'Ro gave the Reverend a good bit of the money he had brought with him from the City of Doom. Phanatik did the same. The Reverend got a little misty-eyed and embraced them both.

REV. RELEVANT: If two men as young as you guys are willing to walk the path of the King with the boldness you just demonstrated back there—it gives me great hope. You two are truly an inspiration. The King told Peter that the church would kick in the very gates of hell. If the King raises up more soldiers like you, it's only a matter of time before those gates come crashing down!

STORYTELLER: The three put their arms around each other in a small circle and prayed. They shook hands and then Kai'Ro and Phanatik went on their way down the Heavenly Highway.

THE CITY OF BABEL-BLING

13

STORYTELLER: After saying goodbye to Reverend Relevant, the two companions continued on their journey. Before long, they saw a familiar face approaching them. It was Preacher.

KAI'RO: Hey, Preacher! It's good to see you.

PREACHER: Likewise. I see that you two finally met up. That's good news.

PHANATIK: Yeah, we've been enjoyin' doin' this thing together. Two are certainly better than one. That's for sure.

PREACHER: Yes, indeed. Listen, I was hoping to catch up with both of you. I know that you've been through a whole lot already. I want you to know that I'm proud of your progress.

KAI'RO: Yes, sir. It hasn't been easy. I mean, I'm not goin' to lie. There's been several times I wanted to quit.

PREACHER: Well, you've made it this far, and that's wonderful news. But I must warn you that you are going to be entering even greater trials still.

PHANATIK: What do you mean?

PREACHER: Not far from here is a great city called the City of Babel-Bling. It's probably the oldest city in the world. You two

126

must pass through there on your way. Most of those who live there are not friendly with the King's soldiers. In fact, most of them hate the King. I wish I could promise you a safe trip, but I can't. I told both of you that there would be trouble and peril on this road, and you've already experienced that personally.

PHANATIK: Yes, sir, we have. I knew what I was gettin' into. I hope the King gives us the strength we'll need, no matter what comes our way.

PREACHER: If you trust in the King with all your heart, He will not disappoint you or fail you. Hold fast to His promises. Cling to His Word.

KAI'RO: Thanks for the heads-up, Preacher.

PREACHER: Go now, my sons, and may the King go with you.

STORYTELLER: Kai'Ro and Phanatik said goodbye to Preacher and walked on together for a while. Then, in my dream, I saw an enormous city just like Preacher had told them. It stretched out almost as far as the eye could see. There were tall skyscrapers shooting up high like great towers, and there were malls and shopping centers scattered everywhere. The buildings had a shine to them as if they were made out of pure diamonds.

Yet, despite the mesmerizing glow, there was a dull grey smog draping over the city like a dirty blanket. Flashy billboards were all along the road as the two travelers drew closer. They had pictures of everything a man or woman could ever want—including fancy cars, jewelry and clothing.

As the two young men reached the town, they were amazed to see how crowded it was. Many people filled the streets, shouting at each other and bumping into one another. The town's people were dressed in all kinds of ways. Some looked like thugs, others like pimps and hustlers. And then there were men and women dressed in pricey business suits. They all hurried in and out of the stores, buying and selling and making a great stir.

When Kai'Ro and Phanatik proceeded down the street, a lot of the people stopped to stare. They had rarely seen guys dressed like them. Some people looked at them with big frowns on their faces. Plenty of people laughed at them and called them some terrible names. A few rough looking guys even came up to Phanatik and shoved him to the ground real hard. They balled up their fists and expected a fight, but Phanatik just got back on his feet.

Kai'Ro put his arm on his friend's shoulder and the two continued to press forward. As they went, people hollered at them and asked them where they were from. The two companions told them, as kindly as they could, that they were pilgrims and strangers in this place. They said they were just passing through on their way to the City of Light. When the people heard this, almost everyone laughed and started to curse at them again, calling them ugly names.

At the same time this was going on, other people were getting in Phanatik and Kai'Ro's faces, waving their goods and begging them to buy the things they were selling. One woman brought out a handful of shiny silver chains and told them how tight they would look if they bought them. Another man dangled the keys to a nice car in front of them. He promised that they would get all the ladies if they just bought one of his rides. A few rough looking guys came up to them and offered them some drugs. Others tried to sell them music and shoes. Even some beautiful looking girls promised them pleasure upon pleasure.

Yet, every time someone offered them another item, Kai'Ro and Phanatik turned away and set their focus on the road ahead. They refused to enter any of their stores or shopping centers. Both felt drawn by different things, but both resisted by reminding each other that none of the things satisfy.

As peacefully and gently as they could, they engaged different people on the streets in conversation. They tried to tell them about the treasures of the King and His City of Light. A few people would listen, but most people tuned them out and then cussed them out. I could tell that Kai'Ro and Phanatik were growing weary with everything that was being shoved in their faces. Finally, Phanatik couldn't take it anymore and hollered out.

PHANATIK: Look, ya'll, we don't *want* what you're sellin'! You feel me? We want the Truth!

STORYTELLER: As soon as he said this, the streets got quiet for a moment and everyone stopped and turned to face the two visitors. Pushing through the crowd, a group of large bouncers from a club called Dancin'-in-the-Dark showed up. Their leader was a strong man named No-Mercy.

NO-MERCY: What'cha talkin' 'bout when you say *the Truth,* fool? You think you got somethin' we don't got? You sayin' that all this stuff we got goin' on in Babel-Bling is a lie or somethin'? Say somethin' before I knock your face in.

STORYTELLER: The group of bouncers and several of the people and store owners gathered around Kai'Ro and Phanatik until there was hardly any space for them to move. No-Mercy got right up in Phanatik's face until their noses were almost touching. His eyes were full of a deep hate, the kind that can snuff a man's life out and never think another thing about it.

PHANATIK: (with courage) All I'm sayin' to ya, brotha, is this. If you and the rest of the people in Babel-Bling think that the stuff you're sellin' and what you got goin' on here is somehow the *real life,* then you're in bondage to a lie. The power and the pleasure that ya'll are pawnin' off here is a joke in comparison to what the King has to offer. Only the King and His Kingdom can offer a brotha the real Life.

STORYTELLER: The whole crowd started shouting and waving their fists at them. A few of the thugs started throwing things at them. Without warning, No-Mercy punched Phanatik in the face with a punch that could have knocked over a tree. Phanatik took off flying back into the crowd and went limp because that blow almost knocked the life out of him. Kai'Ro turned to help his friend, but some of the bouncers and people in the crowd grabbed him and tossed him to the side. No-Mercy grabbed Phanatik by the throat and hit him two more times until Phanatik fell to the ground in a heap.

At this point, the mob grew crazed like sharks when there's blood in the water. Several people, including some of the women, started kicking Phanatik and hitting him. Kai'Ro shook free from the hands and feet holding him down and pushed his way through the crowd. Finally, he was able to crawl on top of his fallen friend and take some of the blows. He cried out in agony as they gave him a savage beating. I thought for sure that both of them would die.

Then I heard some loud whistles, as two men dressed in camouflage burst onto the scene. They were wearing badges and appeared to be some kind of law enforcement. Immediately, the officers started knocking the mob back with their clubs. One of the men was named Corruption and the other was No-Justice. After striking several of the people in their way senseless, they cleared a path to Kai'Ro and Phanatik. Both of them were unconscious and bleeding terribly. The two officers glared at the innocent travelers. Instead of doing anything to help, they just smiled.

CORRUPTION: Now, what in the world happened here to these two guys?

NO-MERCY: Those two fools came into this town and started a riot.

NO-JUSTICE: A riot?

NO-MERCY: Yeah, that's right. They came in here talkin' all this noise about how they were just passin' through on to some City of Light or somethin'. Everywhere they went, they kept yappin' 'bout this King of theirs and how tight He was and all that. They said they were too good for our sorry town. When some of the folks tried to offer them somethin' to buy or do, they'd just turn away.

They came in here actin' all crazy. I mean, look at 'em with that weird Armor they got on. They're clowns, dawg. With all that noise they were talkin' 'bout their City of Light and all that nonsense, man, it got some of us fired up. When that idiot there said he wanted the Truth and that we was all livin' and believin' a lie, well...I just snapped.

CORRUPTION: Looks like we've got some real trouble with these two. We got 'em on a count of questioning the Code of Babel-Bling. We got 'em on disturbing the peace of our town.

NO-JUSTICE: And we got 'em on tellin' people lies and then startin' a riot.

CORRUPTION: I'd like to just leave 'em here and let this mob tear 'em apart.

NO-JUSTICE: Let's haul their sorry carcasses to the Cage. We'll give 'em a trial before Judge Hate-Good and see what happens.

STORYTELLER: The two men dragged Kai'Ro and Phanatik through the road into the center of town. Like animals, they were tossed into two rusted cages. Full of garbage and dried blood, the debris-filled cramped spaces smelled horrible. Many people from the town continued to point at them and mock them. Some hurled bottles at the cages and glass shattered all over their bloodied bodies. Thankfully, both of them had regained consciousness. But they could hardly shield their bodies from the glass and objects thrown at them.

Total chaos had erupted. But on occasion, a few people spoke up and shouted at the crowd. They claimed that Kai'Ro and Phanatik had done nothing wrong. Whenever these people spoke, the crowd cussed them out. Some of them were slapped around and threatened that they'd be thrown in the Cage too if they didn't shut their mouths.

Within a short period of time, another riot broke out as the crowd turned on one another kicking, punching and fighting. Several officers from Corruption and No-Justice's squadron flailed into the mob again, beating them back with their clubs and ordering everyone to calm down.

In the midst of all the disorder, a loud crash like thunder suddenly roared. The multitude grew still and looked up. High above them in an old stone tower stood a tall, thin man. He was dressed in black from head to toe. In his hand, he held a twisted cane with a shiny red skull on the top. His face was shriveled up like a prune and his eyes were hidden behind thick, dark sunglasses. He was none other than Judge Hate-Good, and this was his city.

HATE-GOOD: Silence, you ridiculous fools! Why is there such nonsense going on in my town again? Can you not see that we have the two visitors in the Cage? Do not worry about them any longer. They are in our hands now, and they will receive the justice that is coming to them.

STORYTELLER: A young man in the crowd below named Hopeful shouted out that they had done nothing wrong. He demanded they should be set free. One of Corruption's officers clubbed him from behind and he fell to the ground.

HATE-GOOD: These men will receive a trial for their crimes against our town. We are just. They will get what is coming to them and it will be justice indeed. Arrange the court!

STORYTELLER: Five wooden chairs were set out for five older gentlemen. Like Judge Hate-Good, they also carried crooked canes with red skulls. Their names were Bondage-Maker, Lord-Greed, Blood-Sport, Death-Dealer and Lord-Liar. All of them glared at Kai'Ro and Phanatik who were still slumped in the corners of their cages.

As the men were seated, Phanatik crawled to the edge of his cage and, with a groan of pain, pulled himself up onto his feet.

HATE-GOOD: Do we have witnesses against these men?

CORRUPTION: We do, sir. Our first witness is the owner of "Poison Pawn Shop." His name is Tight Fist.

STORYTELLER: Corruption had Tight Fist place his hand over and swear on a book. On the cover there was a picture of a woman riding a large and ugly red beast.

TIGHT FIST: Yes, I got somethin' to say about these two. They came here talkin' 'bout how all the stuff that we're sellin' in Babel-Bling is goin' to burn one day. They said that we were sellin' and hoardin' up treasure that wasn't goin' to last.

(Pointing an accusing finger) In fact, that one, Phanatik, claimed that we were worshipin' idols and givin' up our souls in exchange for pleasure and treasure. He said if we put our hope in these things that we'd eventually find out they were hopeless. This man had the nerve to say that our belongings would leave our souls when it counted most and that we're in for eternal punishment.

Who does he think he is? This city has been offerin' the stuff he's hatin' on for as long as it's been around. Don't know 'bout ya'll, but I'm *more* than happy with what Babel-Bling has to offer!

STORYTELLER: Most of the people shouted out their agreement and others once again picked up things to throw at the cages.

HATE-GOOD: His words are those of a trouble-making fool. They should be thrashed again just for saying something so stupid and false. Call forward the next witness. We will build our case against them.

CORRUPTION: Our next witness is Twilight. She works at the strip-club, Pleasure Trap.

STORYTELLER: Twilight swore on the book.

TWILIGHT: Yeah, these guys was tellin' me that I had no business doin' what I was doin'. They said that the King made me in His image and that He didn't want me usin' my body for somethin' trashy like dancin'. Last I checked...my body's been mine! They said that I was blinded by the lord of our town, Diablo. And that actually he had me trapped in a lie—a lie that I could use my body anyway I please, as long as it pays the bills.

They told me this King of theirs made me and that *He* owned my body and not me! They even said that none of us really own our bodies and we have no right to do with them whatever we want. I heard 'em say the idea that our bodies are our own is a lie from the pit and Diablo's a son of the devil. In fact, they said I was 'sposed to use my body for this King's glory! Can you believe that?

Then, they started sayin' our hearts are always searchin' for pleasure but the pleasures we're searchin' for is in all the wrong places, and so it won't last. One of 'em said only the King could give us pleasure for real...anything else we were chasin' or doin' that didn't have to do with this King of theirs was totally meaningless and empty. Trust me, when I dance, a lot of guys get pleasure. That's what I do, and yeah, I'm good at it. Who are these two clowns to tell me that my body is some treasure of a King who made me to use it for His glory? They're craaazy!

HATE-GOOD: All these lies! Corruption, it's a wonder you let these men live. I have never heard such filth! Are there any more witnesses?

CORRUPTION: Yes, sir, there is another. His name is Crafty and he's a professor at the University of Random Truths.

STORYTELLER: Like the two before him, Crafty swore with his hand on the evil book.

CRAFTY: Yes, I was amazed at the lies these young men spoke. There has always been a sense of order in our lovely city until these two came along. We learned to tolerate one another and to respect one another's different truths. Our town has always believed that there is no absolute Truth but that we all can live by our own personal truth. Is it not a fact that each of us has found pleasure, purpose and happiness by discovering our own truth?

Yet, these men said there is an absolute Truth, which is greater than all other truths. They said to me and others that the belief that all truths are okay is an illusion and a myth. They said their King is the only Truth and the Truth of His Word has set them free! They claim the truths we believe in are actually lies. When we say life is ultimately about pleasure, about finding our own happiness, and about getting rich and being successful—we are wrong—and these are not truths at all.

They had the audacity to say our University is a joke and this whole town is a joke in comparison to the Kingdom of the King and the Truth of His Kingdom. I heard them say that we are fools to be pitied if we believe our town and what it has to offer is all that there really is.

HATE-GOOD: (shouting) Enough! I have heard enough of this trash. Do we even need another witness?

STORYTELLER: Phanatik grabbed the bars of the Cage and shouted.

PHANATIK: If you are truly a believer in justice, you'll let us at least speak.

HATE-GOOD: If I had my way, I would kill you both now. But you are right. We will hear what you have to say, and then we will give you the justice you deserve. Open the Cage and allow him to speak.

STORYTELLER: When Corruption obeyed Hate-Good's command, Phanatik limped forward. He was still bleeding and his face was bruised and swollen. I noticed that his Armor, as real as it was, did not spare him from the brutal physical blows these people had given him. He had one hand on his right side, holding his ribs. Though he was hurt badly, like a boxer after a one-sided fight, he stood bravely before the huge crowd.

PHANATIK: People of Babel-Bling, I hope you'll listen to what I gotta say. I got Truth for ya'll. I got somethin' you just gotta hear! My name is Phanatik and I'm from the City of Doom. It wasn't so long ago that I felt the same way most of ya'll feel right now. I used to hate the King and everything He stood for.

I mean, when I heard people talk about Him and His words, it used to make me sick. It seemed to me like He wanted to take all the fun out of life. It was nothin' but rules, rules and more rules. Besides, I didn't want anyone tryin' to call the shots in my life. I wanted to do my own thing, you know? I wanted to do *what* I wanted *when* I wanted.

And for the longest that worked for me. I was a hustla'. I made for myself a lot of money and I was able to buy some of the nicer things. Beautiful girls used to crash in my crib. People on my block respected me, and my enemies stayed out of my way. I had everything this world has to offer. I was livin' large!

But over time, it started to lose its effect on me. I mean, it started gettin' harder and harder to feel good the way I wanted. I tried makin' more money. I tried buyin' more rides and even a bigger house. I found more girls and even started usin' some of the stuff I was sellin'. But none of it worked.

Inside, I felt like garbage. I got confused. Why wasn't this stuff makin' me happy no more? Some of you, if you look in your hearts, feel the same way. You're tired of this world and all of its lies. You're tired of chasin' after more and more stuff. Then, as soon as you get it, havin' it just vanish from ya hand like a cloud.

Well, I hit rock bottom, for real. 'Bout that time, I heard 'bout the King. That's when Preacher told me all the stuff I was doin' offended God, the One who made me. What he was sayin' started to click because I was already feelin' real down 'bout all the people I'd hurt, the stuff I'd stolen and the wicked things I'd done. Deep inside I felt real bad, you know? I felt hopeless, for real. Then when Preacher told me that I could have peace with God again if I'd give my life to the King, it gave me real hope.

You see, even though I had all those things, I had no hope. In fact, I was *hope-less*. Lonely. Scared. I'd go to bed some nights and just cry when no one was lookin' or listenin'. It was a big decision for me, but I said goodbye to all the hustlin' and crime. I told some of my homies goodbye too.

It was huge for me when I learned there was treasure in Heaven, in the King's City of Light. It's a treasure that would give me peace—peace that would last for my whole life. This sounded so good to me because all the treasure I had already stored up for myself didn't satisfy me at all.

So, what Tight Fist told ya'll 'bout what I said is true for the most part. If ya'll are puttin' your hope in the treasures of this world, I'm sorry, but they're gonna pass and you're gonna pass away with 'em. You can't take none of this stuff with you. Only the King and His Kingdom will last forever. I decided to flip the script in my life and start chasin' the treasure of the King because I knew it would last.

I don't wanna sound like I'm hatin', but this sorry town is sellin' everybody here a pack of lies. I would beg you not to let this place become your home. My boy Kai'Ro and I realized that this whole world ain't our home no more. I mean, we live here, but the day we gave our lives to the King, that's the day we became citizens of a new family and a new country.

And what Twilight said about me is mostly true too. God made each one of us. We ain't no accident. So, if you're strippin' in clubs, takin' drugs, gettin' drunk, or just tryin' to find the next fix for your body to make it feel good—then you're doin' wrong. I mean, I can't be more plain than that. The King made all of us to honor Him. He gave us talents and abilities so that we could use them for His glory.

Take me, for instance. The King gave me the ability to be a good businessman. I mean, back when I was a shortie, I had mad skills at makin' money. But when I got a little older, I started usin' those skills for evil stuff. I learned that I could make a dime a whole lot quicker if I started dealin' and hustlin'.

It didn't take long before I was one of the richest guys in town. I was listenin' to my own sinful heart and to the lies of Diablo. Don't listen to the lies of Diablo! The prince of this town is a fork-tongued snake that deserves nuttin' but death! He keeps tryin' to convince all of us that our appetites and our desire for pleasure are all that really matter, but it ain't true. We can't find pleasure and happiness until we give our lives to the King!

Let me put it to you like this...when you get tired and thirsty, you go out and buy a sports drink to quench your thirst, right? Well, chasin' pleasures is like chasin' sports drinks. I mean, they'll satisfy you for a moment, but then you gotta get another one the next time you're thirsty. But, guess what, when you get with the King, *He* fills you up and you don't thirst no more. His Kingdom satisfies you, for real. When I gave my life to Him, it was like I didn't need all the other things no more. He became all I needed.

Lastly, I'd like to say somethin' about what Crafty said. Crafty and the dudes like him are all liars. They say that there's all kinda truths out there when it comes to right and wrong, and any one of 'em will lead you to happiness. Don't buy that! The King said there's only one Truth—and He's it! If you don't have Him, then you got nothin'. You'll find yourself holdin' on to an idea or a belief that's really just a lie. It might work for you for a while, but it ends in death.

There are lots of ways that seem right to man, but they all end in death—if they don't line up with the King and what He has to say. I'm cryin' out to ya'll! Hear what I gotta say. Don't settle for what this place is tellin' you and what it's sellin' you. You too can find peace, hope, joy and Life everlasting. It can be yours, if you'll just get outta here and get on the Heavenly Highway. I know some of ya'll hear me.

HATE-GOOD: That's enough! We've heard enough of your garbage! There's no use listening to any more of his pathetic ideas. Do we even need to meet and discuss their verdicts?

BONDAGE-MAKER: No. I have no need to discuss anything. If trash such as these kids doesn't want the freedom and life that this town has to offer, then they don't need to be alive at all. Guilty!

LORD-GREED: If they don't want to get all that they can out of this world, then why be alive? I'm embarrassed that we even let him speak! Guilty on every charge!

BLOOD-SPORT: I would like to see the blood of their bodies spilled on the streets as an example to anyone who dares to believe their lies. Guilty!

DEATH-DEALER: Let them die for blaspheming the name of our lord Diablo and for humiliating our city! If there were more youth like them, can you imagine what would happen to our world? Well, it would fall apart! They are guilty!

LORD-LIAR: I have no patience for pretenders and con artists. Their lies made my ears burn and to look at them makes me sick. I have no doubt that they both are guilty.

STORYTELLER: Kai'Ro stood up in his Cage when he heard all their verdicts. Phanatik never flinched or even looked down. One by one, he stared each of them in their eyes. In my dream, it appeared that a shaft of white light began to shine faintly around him.

HATE-GOOD: There you have it. We have a decision of justice, just as I said we would. These sightless boys had the nerve to call us blind. These liars claimed we didn't know the truth. They told us that we were in bondage and yet they ended up in the Cage. What a funny twist! I believe that the only fitting punishment for these two fools is death. Prepare this one for execution. We will hear him cry out for mercy. But he won't find any.

PHANATIK: I have no fear of you or of these men. It's well with my soul. But you should fear the One who has the power to throw your body and your soul into the pit.

HATE-GOOD: (waving his hand) Finish him off!

STORYTELLER: Corruption, No-Mercy and the other officers rushed forward with their clubs. Then what I saw in my dream caused my heart to break. Those men beat poor Phanatik mercilessly, until he dropped to the ground. They continued to kick and beat him when he was down. Kai'Ro grabbed the bars of his Cage, shaking them and crying out—but no one would listen.

Though the sounds of their clubs assaulting his body grew more sickening with every blow, Phanatik's face was covered with a mysterious peace. He was lying on his back with his eyes fixed towards Heaven. The faint light around him grew brighter and brighter until those in the crowd and those with the weapons had to squint. His lips were moving and I heard him say: "Unless a seed falls into the ground and dies, it remains alone. But if it dies, it bears much fruit."

Several minutes of beating went by until he was almost unrecognizable. Then Hate-Good came down from his tower with a large gun in his hand. The weapon had the words WORLDLY JUDGMENT on it. He pointed it at Phanatik and fired off one sharp shot. Phanatik's body lay still. He was dead. Hate-Good turned to Kai'Ro's Cage and snarled.

HATE-GOOD: Do you see what happened to your friend here? He opened his mouth and filled our town with his filth. You would do well to learn from his mistakes. The City of Babel-Bling shows love to those who love it back, but we hate with all our souls those who follow this King of yours! I think everyone here has learned a lesson today. Do two need to die? Perhaps. Take this man out and thrash him within an inch of his life. Then toss him out of town. I don't think he'll come this way ever again.

STORYTELLER: With that, Hate-Good returned to the stairwell and climbed back up to his tower. Corruption and the others pulled Kai'Ro from the Cage and, like Phanatik, gave him a fierce beating with their clubs. True to their orders, they beat him until he was nearly dead. Then they dragged him out of town and dumped his body along the side of the road. Kai'Ro laid there in a heap, unable to move.

Then I saw one wandering from out of the city. He came out on the road, creeping carefully through the shadows. As he drew closer to Kai'Ro's body, I could see that it was Hopeful.

HOPEFUL 14

STORYTELLER: The night was very dark, and in my dream I saw flashes of lightning. I also heard loud thunder and a fierce rain started to fall. Hopeful stooped down beside Kai'Ro and tried to wake him, but Kai'Ro barely had breath left in him.

HOPEFUL: Man, they messed you up bad. I gotta get you to the doctor, dawg.

STORYTELLER: Hopeful hoisted Kai'Ro up over his shoulder with a great heave. Then he went sloshing down the path as the rain continued to pour and the lightning flashed all around him. Determined, Hopeful went on like this for miles, carrying Kai'Ro because he couldn't carry himself. Finally, a small house appeared on the side of the road. When the lightning flashed, I could see a mailbox that read: "Dr. Mercy."

HOPEFUL: (to himself) Man, I hope the Doc is up, 'cause this boy might not make it through the night.

STORYTELLER: Hopeful made it up to Dr. Mercy's front door and rang the bell. A light came on inside and the door was thrown open. I saw a woman wrapped in a white robe with white slippers on her feet. She was an older woman with a beautiful glow on her face. Her hair was pulled up in a bun. She looked concerned.

MERCY: Oh, my! What has happened to your friend here?

HOPEFUL: Judge Hate-Good and his men beat this brother half to death.

MERCY: For *what*?

HOPEFUL: For nothin', really.

MERCY: He must have had issues with the fact that this young man is one of the King's servants. Won't you come in?

HOPEFUL: (entering the house and laying Kai'Ro on the couch) How'd you know he was one of the King's servants?

MERCY: It's obvious, honey. Look at his Armor. Look at his mark. These things stand out if you have eyes to see. Was there no one with him? It's a perilous road for a soldier to enter Babel-Bling alone.

HOPEFUL: Yes, he had another brotha with him named Phanatik. They killed him. Phanatik spoke like no one I've heard before. He talked as though he and the King were best friends...he sounded like this whole world had nothin' to offer him. It seemed like he knew that he was goin' to die for the King and that didn't bother him at all. I've seen a lot of rough thugs in my life, but I've never seen a guy as brave as him.

STORYTELLER: While Hopeful was speaking, Mercy went to a cabinet and pulled out some bandages and ointments. I saw that one of the bottles of ointment was labeled COMPASSION and the other was called GRACE. Mercy washed Kai'Ro's wounds and treated them with the ointments.

HOPEFUL: I'm sorry, ma'am, but I don't have no money to pay for any of this.

MERCY: Please, son, it's a joy to take in two strangers. If you'd like, there's still some soup on the stove.

HOPEFUL: I appreciate it, but I'm all right. I'd just like to sit here, if that's okay?

MERCY: How old are you, son?

HOPEFUL: I'm fifteen, ma'am.

MERCY: Kind of young to be carrying a battered man around in the dead of night, aren't you? Bet your mom's worried about you.

HOPEFUL: Naw, not really.

MERCY: Every mom worries, son.

HOPEFUL: Not my mom. She ran out on me about five years ago. I haven't seen her for the longest.

MERCY: And your father?

HOPEFUL: He's been locked up since before I was born... killed somebody or somethin'... I don't know.

MERCY: No family?

HOPEFUL: Yeah, if you're countin' the streets as family. Then I got a whole bunch of family.

MERCY: You don't have a single brother or sister... no one at all?

HOPEFUL: My brother's dead. He got shot. My sister's got like three kids from three different men. She lives somewhere over there in Shametown... I don't know. I haven't seen her in the longest either. Like I said, I got some brothas on the streets... we've been together and we're pretty tight.

MERCY: The streets are no kind of family, son. I'm sorry you don't have any flesh and blood to take you in.

HOPEFUL: That's okay. I guess I've just always felt in my heart that things were gonna work out somehow. I've never felt like I just gotta give up or anything like that.

STORYTELLER: Mercy continued to clean and bandage Kai'Ro's wounds. It was a long job and Mercy worked tenderly and carefully. After a while, Kai'Ro started to wake up. The ointments of Compassion and Grace had already taken out a lot of the swelling. Most of the minor cuts and bruises had almost gone away completely.

KAI'RO: Where am I?

HOPEFUL: We're at Mercy's house.

KAI'RO: Who are you?

MERCY: This is Hopeful. He's the young man who saved your life.

KAI'RO: For real? Thanks, brotha.

MERCY: You are fortunate, son, that Hate-Good did not kill you like your friend. It must have been by the good graces of the King that you were spared.

KAI'RO: Yeah, well, I wish it *had* been me. My man, Phanatik, had so much courage out there. I was so scared inside. I could hardly say a word, but it was like he had the words for both of us. Now he's gone!

MERCY: The King takes all of us in our own time, son. Don't be mad because He took your friend and left you behind. Phanatik fulfilled his purpose. The fact that you are still alive is no coincidence. Hate-Good spares no one. This must mean that the King is not finished with what He has for you just yet. You must continue to press on into His plans for your life.

STORYTELLER: Kai'Ro's angry face started to soften. He did his best to sit up on the couch.

KAI'RO: So, Hopeful, what made you come and help me?

HOPEFUL: I guess it's 'cause I felt like you and Phanatik helped me first. I was on the corner at DEATH DRIVE when you and Phanatik started talkin' to some of the dealers on my block. They came at you tryin' to sell you some of their product. Those same guys recruited my older brother when he was about my age. He became one of their local dealers up and down DEATH DRIVE and over there along ADDICT AVENUE. It wasn't more than about two months before my brother got shot dead.

Well, then they started recruitin' me too. But when you two showed up and started talkin' about your King and His Kingdom, it was like you were doin' a whole different kinda recruitin'. The dealers, man, they're recruitin' kids to *die*. But you, you and Phanatik, were recruitin' me and my boys to *Life*. I could feel it stirrin' in me. A lot of guys my age are lookin' for hope in a bad kinda way. For most of us, the gang route and the drug route are the only ways out. But as for me, I've seen too many kids die, get messed up and just disappear. That wasn't no kinda hope for me.

Ya'll spoke with so much passion, dawg! I was just in total awe. I've heard guys talk with passion 'bout who they shot, which girl they got with, how much money they made and all that. But nobody has come on my corner talkin' that way 'bout this King of yours. I guess, for the first time, I started to believe there was a way out for me—a *real* way out.

KAI'RO: Was that you hollerin' out at Hate-Good?

HOPEFUL: (rubbing the knot on the back of his head) Yeah. That was me.

KAI'RO: Well, I appreciate what you did for me. I don't think I would have made it, if you hadn't come to help me out.

MERCY: You would have died if it hadn't been for Hopeful.

HOPEFUL: It's no big deal. Like I said, I feel like you and Phanatik saved *my* life...maybe that means we're even. So, what's next for you?

KAI'RO: Same thing I been doin'. I gotta get back on that Heavenly Highway.

HOPEFUL: Ya think I could roll with you? I mean, I can't go back to Babel-Bling. I got no love for that place no more.

KAI'RO: You need to be in school, brotha. You're too young to be rollin' the streets with no real plans or nothin'. I know of a good school back in Struggle-Town. I met the man who runs it down that way. He'd take you in and even give you a place to stay. You need an education. I dropped out when I was 'bout your age, and I'm not proud of that decision. My brotha, Lil' One, did the same thing and he's been walkin' a dangerous road just like you.

Get you some education and some knowledge about the King's Word. Reverend Relevant, the guy in charge, is a great man and he'll get you on the right path. That man doesn't just talk about the Gospel. He lives the Gospel by bringin' it to the streets.

HOPEFUL: That sounds good. I mean, if this Reverend will take me in, I don't mind goin' back to school.

MERCY: That would be an excellent decision, young man. Your life isn't over just because you have no mom and no dad. That's a tragedy, but don't ever let it be an excuse. The King has plans for you, son, plans to prosper you and not to harm you . . . plans to give you a hope and a future. He's had these plans for you since before you were born. You are still His child and He has wonderful things in store for you.

KAI'RO: Amen.

HOPEFUL: I've never really given up. I know what you're sayin' is true. I mean, my life has been a mess and I've gone through some stuff, but I've always felt like I gotta hang on. A lot of folks in Babel-Bling just give up and check out. But I'm not there yet.

KAI'RO: Sometimes hope gives you just enough ability to hang on. But if you're hangin' on to the King and His Word, then you're hangin' on to somethin' that won't let you down—ever.

HOPEFUL: I feel you on that.

STORYTELLER: The three continued to talk for a while longer until Kai'Ro finally dozed off to sleep. Hopeful fell asleep in an arm chair and Mercy placed a blanket over him. She cleaned up a little bit and then walked over to a rocking chair by the window. Under a dim light, she bowed her head and prayed for the two young men asleep in her living room.

ON THE ROAD AGAIN

STORYTELLER: Kai'Ro and Hopeful spent a few more days with Dr. Mercy. It wasn't long before the doctor's care began to take full effect. The bruises on Kai'Ro's body healed quickly. Soon he was able to get back on his feet and move around again.

During their days together, Kai'Ro wrote a letter for Hopeful to take to Reverend Relevant. They talked a lot about the King and the Heavenly Highway. Then finally, the time came for Kai'Ro to get back on the road.

KAI'RO: I need to thank both of you for puttin' me back together again. The King used you to save me. I owe you a lot of gratitude.

MERCY: No, I should be thanking you, my son. Seeing a young man like you with so much passion for the King and His ways does my heart so much good. I see many hopeless young men and women walk by my place almost every day. Most of them are just busy ruining their lives with violence, drugs, lying and stealing. I don't see too many young soldiers like yourself these days. Instead, there's a lot of young people calling themselves soldiers and trying to act hard. They're trying to pretend that their street life is real life, but actually they're just living a dream.

HOPEFUL: Actually, they're just livin' a *nightmare* and callin' it life. I gotta thank you too. Thanks for lettin' your faith shine like that for me in Babel-Bling. What you and Phanatik showed me was that real courage is actually rebellin' against this world and not conformin' to it. I've seen cats take bullets and beatings out on the streets, but I've never seen nobody take a thrashin' for the King like that. And thanks for pointin' me to Reverend Relevant. You've helped to give me a real shot in life.

STORYTELLER: The three took turns giving each other hugs. Then Hopeful said goodbye and took off with his letter from Kai'Ro.

MERCY: I saw what you did for that boy, and I think the King is going to use you to reach a lot of these young people.

KAI'RO: What do you mean?

MERCY: You became a hero to Hopeful over the past few days. Now, I'm not talking about the kind of hero you see on TV with all the money and the celebrity and all that. Most of those people aren't heroes. He saw the Life of the King inside of you and it became something he wanted. He saw that you were walking in a way that he had only heard other people talking about. That made a powerful impact on him. I think the King is going to call you back to where you came from.

KAI'RO: With all respect, ma'am, I'm never goin' back to the City of Doom. I can't go back that way again.

MERCY: I think you missed my meaning, son. It's obvious that you're no longer the young man who once lived in that city. There's no way you'd go back there and return to your old ways. I believe that. But the city *needs* the Truth that you have now. *That* is what I am saying. It needs a soldier to point the way to the Highway—to point the way to the King.

I have a feeling if you went back to your old neighborhood, they'd hardly recognize you. Sure, they'd recognize your face, but they wouldn't recognize your soul. And your soul says a whole lot more about you than anything else. Like Hopeful, I think there are some young people who would listen. I think there are a whole lot of folks who are thirsting inside for something that's real... for hope... for Life.

KAI'RO: I don't know, I guess I never really thought about it like that. For me, I've just been tryin' to get to the City of Light and just make sure that I stay on the Heavenly Highway. Along the way, I figured I'd just tell people about the King.

MERCY: Well, that works too, but I think the King may send you back to your old city, to your old block and to your old friends. You need to pray on it, because that may be what He has for you.

KAI'RO: Yes, ma'am. I'll pray on it. Thank you again. I best be goin'.

STORYTELLER: Kai'Ro set out on the road again. As he moved, I could see a difference in him that was remarkable. His face was alive with peace, wisdom and strength. I no longer saw the fear and insecurity that had been there before. His Armor was dented and banged up. There were battle scars on his body. But he walked like a warrior on a mission. To me, he seemed like a man from a whole different world altogether.

After he traveled on for a distance, I saw a gigantic gold and white tent off to the side of the road. From the top of the tent, a flag was flapping in the wind with the words CIRCUS OF WISDOM on it.

Kai'Ro stopped for a moment to see what was going on. Just outside the Circus entrance stood a tall and beautiful woman wearing a black top hat. She was older, but she was radiant looking. Her hair was long and pulled into a ponytail. She wore a flashy gold blouse with a flowing white cape that made her look like the Mistress of Ceremonies. Holding a large megaphone up to her mouth, the woman hollered out to a large crowd gathered just outside of the Circus.

SOPHIA: How long will you simple ones keep loving your simple ways? How long are you mockers going to keep on mocking? *Idiots!* How long will you refuse to learn? Turn to me and I can change your life! Look, I'm ready to pour out my spirit on you and tell you all I know. I've been calling you, but you walk right past as if you're deaf. When I've reached out to you, you just shove me away.

STORYTELLER: Most of the crowd ignored her. A few threw ugly hand gestures in her direction, and others just laughed as she continued to cry out. Kai'Ro, who was curious, drew closer and started to push his way through the crowd. As he did so, Sophia shouted out again.

SOPHIA: Since you laugh at what I'm saying and make jokes about my advice, how can I take you seriously? I'll turn the tables and joke about your troubles! What if the roof falls in and your whole life goes to pieces? What if drama strikes and there's nothing to show for your life but rubble and ashes? You'll need me then. You'll call for me—but don't expect an answer. No matter how hard you look, you won't find me!

STORYTELLER: Kai'Ro kept pushing his way through the crowd. They were packed tightly. Many of those around him were sipping drinks out of paper bags. Some were arguing with one another. Others appeared to be gambling and fighting. As Kai'Ro reached the tent's entrance, Sophia saw him and smiled. It seemed like she had known he was coming.

SOPHIA: Traveler! Do you seek wisdom? Do you desire to gain insight on how to live your life? Would you like illumination to help you understand the world around you?

KAI'RO: Yes, ma'am. I would.

SOPHIA: Then you have come to the right place. There is so much to show you. Come inside with me.

STORYTELLER: Sophia pulled back one of the large flaps and welcomed him into the tent. Inside was a shocking scene. The first room they entered was called PERSPECTIVE PLACE. It was a small room with several people walking around. But everything was upside down and they were walking on the ceiling!

KAI'RO: Whoa! What's goin' on here?

SOPHIA: Strange, isn't it?

STORYTELLER: Kai'Ro stopped and rubbed his eyes to make sure he wasn't seeing things.

KAI'RO: Why are they all walkin' around in the air like that?

SOPHIA: Are you sure that *you're* not the one walking around in the air?

KAI'RO: Huh?

STORYTELLER: Kai'Ro looked down at his feet and saw that they were actually suspended in midair. His jaw dropped. He looked up at the people above him and saw that they were actually walking around on the ground.

KAI'RO: What in the world is goin' on here? Am I trippin' or some-thin'?

SOPHIA: No, sweetheart, you are learning your first valuable lesson. The wisdom of the King comes from the Upside-Down Kingdom. His ways are higher than our ways, and His thoughts are higher than our thoughts. When you begin to see the world through the wisdom of the King, then everything around you looks like foolishness. But, you must also understand this. If you walk by the King's wisdom, you will appear foolish to those who walk by the wisdom of the world.

STORYTELLER: Just then, those above Kai'Ro started to point at him and laugh. They made crude jokes about him and called him names.

SOPHIA: You see, in the same way, the world mocked and persecuted the King when He walked the earth. They didn't understand Him or what He came to do. The King made it clear to His followers that—just like the world misunderstood and hated Him—the world would misunderstand and hate everyone who followed Him.

KAI'RO: This just feels weird to me.

SOPHIA: It takes getting used to, but eventually you'll understand that what is right-side up is actually upside down. I'm sure you've already started to experience this on your journey.

KAI'RO: Yeah, when you mention it that way. I've talked to a lot of different folks, and many of 'em just don't seem to get it. I guess it's like what they're actually callin' truth and reality is in fact an illusion or somethin'.

SOPHIA: Yes. Let me show you something else that may help you better understand this principle of upside down being the right way.

STORYTELLER: Sophia took Kai'Ro into another part of the tent. They walked into a wide arena with a large, sandy pit in the middle. The place was packed with people, and Sophia sat down in one of the two remaining seats. She asked Kai'Ro to sit down next to her. Just then, a large, barrel-chested man stepped out into the center of the sand pit with a microphone. The arena went dark and only a bright spotlight shone down on the man in the center of the ring.

ANNOUNCER: Ladies and gentlemen, I present to you an amazing battle of overwhelming odds. You are about to witness something extraordinary. Hold your breath and do not be frightened as I unleash the gigantic, monstrous, bigger than life—killer—*Crusher!*

STORYTELLER: The spotlight then swung its beam to a different part of the ring. To everyone's surprise, a large metal door opened with a loud bang. After that, a giant of a man came running out, roaring like a wild animal. In his hand was the largest Louisville slugger bat I've ever seen. The gigantic man was nearly nine feet tall and every inch of his body was covered in rippling muscles. He growled and beat his chest with his hands. Many in the crowd shrieked and some even covered their eyes in fear.

KAI'RO: I've never seen a guy as big as that dude before. He's like a giant.

ANNOUNCER: And now, I present to you his competition. The humble, the tiny, the microscopic, the almost-so-small-you-might-miss-him—*Mighty Mite!*

STORYTELLER: The light swung again to the opposite side of the ring. Out of a small, wooden door emerged a little man wearing some armor that appeared to be too big for him. He ran out into the ring with his little legs pumping as fast as they could go. In one hand, he held a tiny shield with a large red cross on it. In his other hand was a tiny dagger. When he stepped into the center of the ring, the crowd erupted into boos and people shook their heads in disbelief.

KAI'RO: Man, this is gonna be a slaughter. Someone needs to get that lil' man out of there, or they're gonna be sendin' him home to his family in a soup can.

SOPHIA: Wait and see, child.

STORYTELLER: Crusher glared at Mighty Mite and his nostrils were flaring like a bull's before it charges. Mighty Mite closed his eyes and appeared to say a short prayer. Then he lowered the visor on his helmet.

ANNOUNCER: Let the battle begin!

STORYTELLER: Crusher let out another bone-chilling roar and took a great swing at Mighty Mite. But the little man rolled to the side and the bat swung over his body with a loud whoosh. Crusher cursed and pounded the bat into the ground again and again, but Mighty Mite continued to roll ahead of his swings and out of harm's way. This went on for some time and the crowd grew restless. People started chanting and booing again.

Finally, Mighty Mite rose to his feet and dodged another great swing from the giant of a man. Crusher took another cut that could have knocked over a building, but this time Mighty Mite ducked and rolled between his challenger's legs. Then with a quick stroke, the tiny man stuck the giant in the rear-end with his tiny dagger. Crusher howled and jumped in the air like a child who accidentally sat down on a bee. Several in the crowd burst into laughter.

Crusher's eyes grew red, as he looked at his small opponent with sheer hatred. He gripped his bat with two hands and took another powerful swing. To everyone's surprise, Mighty Mite did not move. The bat struck him in the head with such force that the entire arena shook as if rocked by an explosion. Kai'Ro put his head in his hands.

KAI'RO: I can't watch this.

SOPHIA: (putting her hand gently on his shoulder) Look again, son.

STORYTELLER: Kai'Ro looked up slowly and could not believe what he saw. Mighty Mite was still standing in the same place and Crusher was holding the nub of a broken bat. The pieces of his slugger were scattered all over the arena. Everyone in the audience was shocked. Crusher looked shocked as well. He snarled, balled up one of his mighty fists and punched it into Mighty Mite's chest. It was a blow that could break bricks. Instead, the arena was filled with the horrible sound of the bones in his hands being cracked and crushed to bits. Crusher screamed in pain.

At this point, the crowd began to cheer: "Might-ee Mite! Might-ee Mite!" This only made Crusher even angrier. With his good hand, he tried to lift Mighty Mite off of the ground, but he couldn't. Frustrated, he kicked his tiny opponent. Once again, nothing happened except the crunching of his toes. Now he hopped around on one foot, howling and yelling. The crowd burst into laughter and started cheering again. Crusher lost his balance and fell into the sand.

Mighty Mite sprang onto Crusher's chest like a lion on its prey. He raised his dagger for a finishing blow, and the crowd urged him to finish the fight. They chanted: "Kill him! Kill him!" The little man thrust his blade down for a finishing blow. But just before he buried it in his opponent's chest, the dagger burst into a beautiful bouquet of flowers. Mighty Mite held it high above his head in triumph, and the crowd erupted into cheers that became almost deafening.

The tiny man pointed towards Heaven as the lights suddenly went out. Then, as quickly as they went out, they came on again. But when they did, Kai'Ro was alone with Sophia in an empty arena.

SOPHIA: What did you see here, son?

KAI'RO: Well, I learned that I need to get some of that lil' man's armor because that stuff is the real deal. Naw, I'm just playin'. I learned that the biggest and the baddest don't always win. That Crusher guy was the strongest and meanest man I've ever seen in my life. There was no way that he shoulda lost that fight...no way.

SOPHIA: So, how did he lose?

KAI'RO: He was too prideful. It was like he believed that, just because he was bigger and stronger, he was guaranteed to win. He obviously didn't have what it takes even though it seemed like he did, even to me.

SOPHIA: And did Mighty Mite have what it takes?

KAI'RO: Yes, ma'am, he obviously had what it took to beat that monster. I mean, he took a savage beating. But the more he took, the more it embarrassed and humiliated Crusher. It was like Crusher ended up lookin' like a complete fool in the end. I mean, he got dogged out for real out there.

SOPHIA: The King uses the weak to shame the strong. In His Kingdom, even things that are low and despised shame the things that are high and mighty. Why do you think He does this?

KAI'RO: So no man can boast, I guess. I mean, Mighty Mite obviously had someone bigger than him fightin' that battle for him. There's no way he should have won that one. No way.

SOPHIA: Kai'Ro, the world wants to impress upon you the power of human strength, riches and success. The worldly view is to continually boast in what it has and what it does. But the King desires that you boast in the fact that you know Him. He wants you to proclaim to everyone that you know He is living *in* and *through* you. This is your greatest boast.

In fact, all of the King's servants are Mighty Mites. There are no "super-servants" who do anything great outside of what He allows and provides. At the same time, the King shames the powers of this world by bringing those powers crashing down through the small and weak. Think about the young boy, David, who killed a giant like Crusher. Not only that, the King Himself choose a small group of fishermen, a tax collector and a couple political hotheads. With them, He built a team that shook the earth.

It's this way. When the King writes a story, He gets all the credit. That's because He's the King and He deserves it. As a Lover of impossible stories, He allows things like Mighty Mite's impossible victory over Crusher to become a reality. We have no choice but to sit back and say in awe, "Only the King could do that." When you seek to give Him the glory in all that you do, He will use you to topple the mighty and strong.

KAI'RO: That's deep.

SOPHIA: Yes, that's the Upside-Down Kingdom. The King uses midgets to knock down mountains, whispers to silence storms and nobodies to change the world . . .

KAI'RO: You mean, even little nobodies like me?

SOPHIA: (smiling) Yes. Even little nobodies like you, son.

STORYTELLER: As soon as she said that, there was a loud honking noise, and a strange looking car drove out into the center of the sand pit. It was covered in many different colors, as if someone had just taken various buckets of paint and sloshed them all over it. Because the wheels were all different sizes, they wobbled as if they were about to come off.

The little car drove around in circles twice with a large plume of black smoke shooting out of the tailpipe. When it stopped, one of the side doors opened. A clown stepped out wearing a big orange wig with a funny hat sitting on top of it. He had on a bright red clown nose and his face was covered with white paint. His cheeks were round and rosy. He waddled out with large, floppy shoes and walked over to a small wooden chair in the center of the ring.

Then the clown sat down and pulled out a big Bible. He laid it in his lap and started to read. Just then a loud sound of bass pounded into the arena as a black Bentley pulled into the ring. The glass was tinted dark and its silver rims sparkled. The Bentley circled around the clown and his little car once and then came to a halt.

The doors were thrown open and four rough looking guys stepped out. They were all dressed in baggy jeans with long white tall-Ts. Shiny gold chains hung around their necks, and clean white and blue Air Force Ones were on their feet. The driver, Flash, was smoking a large brown cigar. When the thugs saw the clown reading his Bible, Flash pointed at him and took a step towards him.

FLASH: Yo, ya'll check out this clown here! I know him. He lives like three doors down from me. This dude is a loser, for real!

STORYTELLER: The gang of thugs surrounded the clown and took turns harassing him.

THRILLS: What'cha doin', payaso? Sittin' there in that retarded outfit you got there, ese?

CASH: Look at this fool...just sittin' there like some kinda geek, readin' that Book of his.

ICE: I've never seen someone look so stupid before.

STORYTELLER: The clown looked up at them for a moment but then returned to reading his Bible.

THRILLS: (holding a bottle of cerveza) Hey, ese, why don't you come to any of the parties, payaso? I don't see you at none of the clubs. You one of them holy santos who's too good for everyone? Ain't you into the party scene...the girls, the cerveza, the thrills, homie?

STORYTELLER: The clown looked up at Thrills and shook his head.

ICE: Why don't you have no nice clothes, homie? Man! Ain't you got no ice, no shoes, no nothin'? You got anything nicer than that clown suit, fool? 'Cause those clothes you got on is lame!

STORYTELLER: The four young men burst into laughter. The clown shook his head again. Cash took out a wad of hundred dollar bills and ruffled them in the clown's face.

CASH: You got a stash like this, clown? You got the green and the muscle to make things happen?

STORYTELLER: This time, the clown just smiled and shook his head.

FLASH: (blowing smoke from his cigar) Naw, homies, he's got nothin'! He's just a clown, that's all. He's just a lame ol', Bible-followin', King-lovin', too broke, too lame, too weak, good-for-nothin' clown!

STORYTELLER: Flash pulled out a black gun from the back of his pants and held it up to the clown's head.

FLASH: Don't know 'bout ya'll, but I hate clowns! The world would be a better place without clowns like this fool.

STORYTELLER: He was about to pull the trigger. But just then, a small fire engine burst into the arena with its siren blaring. On the side of the fire engine were the words KING'S PERSPECTIVE. Flash and his crew looked at the fire engine in shock. Suddenly, the truck shot out a hard burst of water that doused them all. It was a powerful blast and, for a while, Kai'Ro couldn't see what was going on.

After the mist cleared and the fire engine drove away, there was a new scene before him. A young man, who looked a whole lot like Kai'Ro, sat on a bench with his Bible. He had on jeans and a T-shirt and a simple cross hung from his neck.

Standing around the bench were four clowns. All four were dumpy and goofy looking in their appearance. Their crisp jeans and fresh Ts were replaced with skin-tight polka-dot pants and fluffy, frilly, polka-dot shirts. On their feet were Air Force Ones, but they were oversized and floppy with bright pink shoelaces. The jewelry around their necks was clunky and made of plastic, with big rocks inside. It was so heavy that it nearly pulled them over.

THRILLS: (holding a baby bottle) Man, what happened to us, ese?

STORYTELLER: Ice tried to say something, but there was a huge pacifier in his mouth. Flash looked at his hand and saw that he was holding a big plastic gun that shot bubbles. Cash glanced at his wad of money and was shocked to see a handful of large Monopoly game bills.

CASH: Man, I'm flat broke, homie. This won't buy me nothin'!

FLASH: (puffing on his cigar and looking at his bubble gun) Shoot, this ain't right, ya'll. This ain't right!

STORYTELLER: Just then, Flash's cigar exploded with a crack and covered his face with soot.

FLASH: Man, let's get outta here, dawg. This is craaazy!

STORYTELLER: The four "gangsta" clowns waddled as fast as they could to get back to their Bentley, but the Bentley was gone. In its place was a rusted and ugly bicycle with four seats on it.

THRILLS: I ain't fixin' to ride on that thing, homie.

FLASH: Man, get yoself on that bike. We gotta get out of here!

STORYTELLER: The four clowns jumped on the bike and pedaled away. The tires were very wobbly and the clowns crashed three times before they finally made it to a tunnel and disappeared.

KAI'RO: Why do the nations rage and the people plot in vain?

SOPHIA: The kings of the earth set themselves, and the rulers take counsel together against the King and against His Anointed One . . .

KAI'RO: The One Who sits in the heavens *laughs*. The King laughs at these clowns until his stomach hurts . . .

SOPHIA: This is good. You know the King's Letters. Most of the world calls the King's followers clowns, and they do everything to make fun of the King's people. They think that those who identify with the King and take His ways seriously are no better than fools.

KAI'RO: Yeah, but the King makes the final call. Anyone who starts cheering about this world and the power and pleasure it offers is the *clown*! That type of person is fooled. We've got clowns on the radio, clowns in the videos, clowns signing record deals, and clowns in the movies.

SOPHIA: But again, it's only in the Upside-Down Kingdom that you can see they're the clowns. These clowns try to mask their foolishness behind sunglasses, jewelry, expensive cars, racy videos, parties and clothing. But the King is coming back! And when He does, He will strip them of all their imaginary power and reveal them to everyone around as the clowns they truly are. What a sad and humiliating day that will be! Come on, there is still more to see.

STORYTELLER: Sophia took Kai'Ro by the hand and led him into another part of the Circus. In this next room there was a tall man with a long mustache. He had on bright suspenders and a bowler hat. On his suspenders was a button that read: MR. OPPORTUNITY.

In front of him was a large crowd of people from all over the world. They were gathered together and waiting for something to happen. Behind him, and to his left, were three booths. To his right was a large open plot of ground that looked like a garden.

MR. OPPORTUNITY: Step right up, ladies and gentlemen! Don't be shy! Come here, get your LIFE and get ready to use it any way that you please!

STORYTELLER: The eager crowd filed into a large line and Mr. Opportunity handed each of them a green ticket with the word LIFE written on it. Every single person in that line received one ticket.

In back of Mr. Opportunity were more vendors who hollered to the crowds. To his left were three "bottle toss" booths. One booth was called The Blame Booth. One was called The Booth of Entitlement, and the last one was called The Booth for Quick Fixes. The people operating these booths were sneaky looking characters who hollered to the crowd as soon as they walked over with their LIFE ticket.

VENDOR ONE: Come to The Blame Booth. Have you had a hard life? Maybe a no-good family? Do you have a horrible job? Perhaps you've grown up in a bad neighborhood or go to a really bad school! Or, wait...maybe you're a victim of the government or some unfair system. Step up to my booth, ladies and gentlemen! Give me your LIFE and I'll give you one shot...one lucky shot. We have terrific door prizes that we're just anxious to give away, so come on! What'cha say? Give me your LIFE and give it a toss!

VENDOR TWO: Ladies and gentlemen, step up to The Booth of Entitlement! Do you have unresolved problems? Are people not meeting your needs? Who's going to solve your issues? Why is no one giving you what's rightfully yours? Who's putting unrealistic expectations on you? Give me your LIFE and I will give you one toss. You won't believe the door prizes I have waiting for you.

VENDOR THREE: Who needs a Quick Fix? Do you, sir? Surely you do, ma'am! Line up! Line up! That's it! That's it! Give me your LIFE! This is a no-brainer. I'll give you one shot! You knock down the bottles and I'll give you all kinds of pleasures and thrills. There's no need to strain or struggle for anything. Just give me your LIFE and I guarantee you'll walk away with something grand!

STORYTELLER: All three booths displayed large, fat bottles that almost anyone could hit. It looked like an easy way to win a prize. Many of those with their LIFE tickets started to line up at the various booths, as the Vendors continued to holler at them to come and spend their LIFE. There was no real rhyme or reason to who stood in line, because I saw people from every race and language. There were the rich and poor, the clothed and nearly naked.

Then I looked to the right. An old man in overalls named Farmer Diligence hollered to those with their LIFE tickets to step up and buy a bag of seeds. Above his head was an old wooden sign that read, THE GARDEN OF COMMUNITY AND RE-SPONSIBILITY.

FARMER DILIGENCE: Give me your LIFE and I'll give you a bag of seeds. You can come and step up into the Garden, dig in the dirt, plant your seeds, and watch 'em grow. It's a long-term investment, but I promise there'll be fruit for ya. Don't waste your LIFE blamin' people, tryin' to get others to do for you what you should do for yourself, or seekin' a quick fix for somethin' that won't last.

STORYTELLER: A few people stopped and some even exchanged their LIFE ticket for a small sack of seeds, a shovel, and a watering can. Many of those in the crowd who were trying to make up their mind looked back at the booths once they saw that the people in the Garden were doing some really hard work. Some mumbled that the booths seemed much easier and made more sense.

I saw in my dream that almost everyone who threw one of the balls at the bottles hit the mark and sent the bottles soaring with a great crash. Every time they exploded, the crowd roared in excitement. The Vendors then filled the winners' hands with shiny tokens. On each token different words were written: FLEETING PLEASURE, UNEARNED WAGES, SMALL COMFORT, MEANINGLESSNESS, BITTERNESS and FRUSTRATION. Although very eager to get them, I noticed that the winners took very little time to really *look* at the tokens.

The Vendors asked them to move on quickly to another booth called the Payout Booth in the back corner. There, they could cash in their tokens for their door prize. The people went with excitement on their faces and handed their coins to the Payout Clerk. She smiled at them, reached behind a counter and pulled out a wilted and dying potted plant. Each winner received one. But everyone who received the prize protested.

The Clerk laughed at them and told them that they got just what they deserved.

CLERK: What did you expect, you sad fools? Did you really think that gambling your LIFE away on Blame, Entitlement and Quick Fixes would somehow win you something special? I'm sorry, but a LIFE wasted on those things will be fruitless and dead.

STORYTELLER: One at a time, the disappointed winners slowly walked away. Some went away crying. Others went away cursing. Still others just sat down and stared at the useless plant in their hands.

KAI'RO: Shoot! That's messed up! Those poor people got hoodwinked and now they got nothin' to show for it.

SOPHIA: Yes, Kai'Ro, it's a horrible ending to a wasted LIFE, but those unfortunate people reaped what they sowed. Now, take another glance at the Garden.

STORYTELLER: Back at the Garden, something interesting was happening. Those who had tilled the soil, planted, and watered their seeds were all staring at the ground. All of them were sweaty and dirty and I noticed how everyone had aged to varying degrees. As they watched the ground, little green shoots started to push up through the soil. The plants grew quickly until each of them became strong, gorgeous trees. The limbs were full of pretty flowers and various kinds of lush fruit. All the people cheered and hugged one another.

As they plucked fruit from the limbs, there were different words on each piece. Words like HOPE, PURPOSE, MEANING, DAILY BREAD, PEACE and DIRECTION. The fruit looked delicious, and those in the Garden took the whole day to enjoy it. Then, to my surprise, one person with a lot of fruit noticed the crowd of people outside who were stuck with their dead plants. He motioned to others in the Garden and they started handing out armfuls of the fruit, offering HOPE, PURPOSE, MEANING,

DAILY BREAD, PEACE and DIRECTION to those who had nothing.

Some of those who had wasted their LIFE at the booth gladly and joyously accepted the fruit. But others shoved it away and clung to their dead plant as if they were somehow proud of it.

SOPHIA: Do you understand the meaning of all this, Kai'Ro?

KAI'RO: Whew! There's a lot going on here...but I'll give it a shot. Everyone gets a LIFE. We all got that in common...and LIFE is an *opportunity*. Even though we all get a LIFE, our lives aren't all the same. When I checked out that crowd, I saw people from everywhere. There were some who looked like they hadn't eaten in weeks. And there were some who looked like they hadn't stopped eating in weeks. I saw bums and I saw millionaires. There were people who talked educated and people who talked like they hadn't spent a day in school.

I guess everybody had an opportunity to spend their LIFE on somethin'. Seems to me like the people who wanted the least amount of struggle chose those booths. They thought it'd be easier to blame folks and try to get some quick results.

SOPHIA: Why is that such a temptation, and why do you think most people chose those booths?

KAI'RO: Well...I mean, it's just that most people are gonna take the easy road. Besides, hittin' those bottles was a surefire thing. A baby could hit them. I remember growin' up as a kid, I used to blame just about everyone and everything for my problems. Even when I got in trouble, it was somebody else's fault.

It seems to feel better when you can convince yourself that your problems aren't your fault. And quick fixes...that's an easy one. I found out in my neighborhood that I could make a dime a whole lot faster hustlin' on the streets rather than goin' to school or workin' a job. That's common sense on the street—make a dime or get a thrill as quick 'n easy as possible.

SOPHIA: Let's talk about Entitlement for a minute. Do you remember the story of God's children in Egypt?

KAI'RO: Yeah, they were slaves in Egypt for like four hundred years.

SOPHIA: Yes, and God in His goodness delivered them from bondage through a series of miracles. To save their lives, He struck down the most powerful man in the world along with his army. Then God led His people with a cloud by day and a fire by night. Through amazing miracles, He brought them food. Still, it wasn't long before the people started complaining and grumbling. They grew tired of the food God provided and felt that they were entitled to something better. They grew thirsty and started whining about the lack of water. When He gave them water, they didn't like the taste.

Eventually, they even said they'd settle for going back to slavery in Egypt rather than following God. They wanted Him to fix every problem and satisfy their every desire. But as soon as He did that, they just wanted more.

This is an age-old problem in the world. A lot of people grow up believing that someone else should solve all their problems. They point at the government, their parents, the church, their schools or their neighbors. If those people or organizations don't provide for them and solve all their issues, they whine and cry. Then, when various organizations step up to help, there is usually gratitude at first, but most people soon begin to feel like they have a *right* to those things. The entitlement syndrome sets in and becomes something that cripples people from advancing in life.

Again, this is a problem that goes back to the beginning of time. It's a problem that has spread all over the earth and has taken root in the hearts and lives of people.

KAI'RO: You're right. You see this attitude everywhere in our country, in the hood and in the 'burbs. A lot of folks just think, "Hey, somebody else needs to fix or solve my problems."

SOPHIA: As I said to you earlier, the King's Word is true. You will reap what you sow. The people who *chose* the booths *chose* to sow their LIFE into something that bears no fruit. As a result, their choice brought them death and meaninglessness in the end. A study of people throughout history will show you that anyone who has chosen BLAME, ENTITLEMENT or QUICK FIXES for their LIFE ends up in misery, pain, disappointment and death. Wisdom says to *look* at the past and to *watch* those around you, so that you don't repeat their mistakes.

KAI'RO: Word.

SOPHIA: What about the Garden? What did you see there? Why did so few go?

KAI'RO: (laughing) That was a lot of work. Those folks were sweatin' and gettin' dirty, for real. Someone comes up to me and says, "Hey, you can throw this ball and win a prize. Or you can work hard in the hot sun and plant some seeds." What'cha think I'm gonna say? But really, the people in the Garden seemed to see their LIFE as more of an investment than a gamble. They were lookin' for some long-term results.

SOPHIA: The Garden of Community and Responsibility. What do you think about that name?

KAI'RO: Well, RESPONSIBILITY is a key starting point to LIFE. Like you said, everyone in the world grows up on a different part of the block, so to speak. I mean, some of us grew up in the hood and some grew up in the 'burbs. There's those who grew up in a mansion with plenty of food and some that grew up in a grass hut with nothin' but bugs.

But the Truth is, we all received a LIFE from the King—and that's a gift. My life growin' up was nothin' to celebrate. I mean, I grew up broke and in a home with a lot of chaos and pain. There were folks miles down the road in the 'burbs who had it good, ya know. They had the nice house with the two-car garage. They went to good schools and had good families for the most part. I could see the difference between their lives and mine, and I would use those differences as an excuse.

Because I spent all my time blamin' people, blamin' my circumstances and whinin' for others to solve my problems, I was truly stuck. At some point, I had to take RESPONSIBILITY for myself. For me, the starting point was taking RESPONSIBILITY for my own sin and mistakes. It meant making the RESPONSIBLE decision of giving my LIFE to the King and gettin' myself on the Heavenly Highway.

SOPHIA: Yes, that's the most important first decision.

KAI'RO: But it don't stop there. That's just where it all *begins*. Yeah, I had to deal with a sorry school system and a lousy home, but so do a lot of people all over the world. In fact, there's a lot of folks who got it much worse. I never finished school, but I'm goin' back to get my GED. I can't allow all the drama and chaos in my life to be an excuse for not movin' forward. It's time for me to take some RESPONSIBILITY for myself and, by the King's grace, start takin' some leaps forward in my LIFE. Having RESPONSIBILITY is an investment in yourself. It's an investment in excellence.

SOPHIA: And perhaps an investment in your own future.

KAI'RO: Yeah. Responsibility is not just for *you*—it's about your future family, your kids and maybe even your grandkids. I mean, I've started to see the importance of hard work. I never had no man in the house who held down a job and showed me the importance of providin' for his family. In fact, most of the guys who were in and out of my life provided for themselves by stealin' and hustlin'. That's how I learned to survive.

But you know, the King said that those who steal should steal no longer, but should learn to work with their own hands. He even said that if somebody doesn't provide for his own, particularly those in his own household, he has denied the faith and he's worse than an unbeliever. I don't ever want my kids to think that it's normal for dads to dip out of the house, run the streets, get fired from every job and shack up with other women. I don't want my son growin' up thinkin' that it's okay to take the easy road of crime to make ends meet.

My dad passed nothin' on to me but a legacy of brokenness and abandonment. But that doesn't mean that I have to pass that same thing on to my kids. I'm gonna show 'em that a man leads by holdin' down a job, by comin' home each night and by stayin' faithful to his wife. At some point, somebody has to be responsible by steppin' on the brakes and saying, "Enough is enough." My family has been skiddin' down the road for as long as I can remember. Not no more. By the King's grace, I'm goin' to put a stop to all that.

SOPHIA: (smiling) You are starting to see upside down, my child.

KAI'RO: Yeah, and COMMUNITY is crucial too. We got some lousy and hurtin' neighborhoods. I grew up in one. But I gotta be honest. We got a lousy and hurtin' nation. Shoot, we got a lousy and hurtin' world. Right now, most of us are too worried about ourselves and our own lil' worlds. COMMUNITY is all about worryin' about your neighbor and her needs and her hurts. It's about teamin' up with one another to make your streets livable again. It's about grabbin' a hammer and puttin' together the walls that have come down and jackin' up the foundation on places that have sunk in the mud.

SOPHIA: Yes! Yes! It's about loving your neighbor as much as yourself and about putting their needs before your own. Instead of demanding assistance for yourself, you give a helping hand to someone else. Instead of complaining about how you only have five pairs of shoes, you give away four pairs to four people who have no shoes. You do this for your next-door neighbor—but also for your neighbor on the other side of the world!

KAI'RO: It's all about changin' the world, one block at a time . . .

SOPHIA: One block at a time. *Exactly!* It's simple and you've got it. I want you to understand two important facts in all of this. For one, the importance of investing your LIFE in RESPONSIBILITY and COMMUNITY are the King's principles. Notice the fruit to be reaped: HOPE, PURPOSE, MEANING, DAILY BREAD, PEACE and DIRECTION. It's not necessarily an investment that's going to get you more money. But can you put a price tag on a life full of MEANING and HOPE? Who wouldn't want those things in their life?

Amazingly, even someone who doesn't know or follow the King, but gives his life to RESPONSIBILITY and COMMUNITY, will still reap the fruits of HOPE, PURPOSE, MEANING, DAILY BREAD, PEACE and DIRECTION. They will obviously be in much smaller portions than one who knows and follows the King, but these are Kingdom principles that are good for followers and non-followers alike. The King's principles work regardless of who applies them. This is an amazing Truth.

What is equally true is that even followers of the King will receive FLEETING PLEASURE, UNEARNED WAGES, SMALL COMFORT, MEANINGLESSNESS, BITTERNESS and FRUSTRATION if they choose to invest their LIVES in BLAME, ENTITLEMENT and QUICK FIXES. The fruit of fleshly living and following the world's system will produce the same fruit, which is *nothing—* even in the lives of the King's followers. *Be aware of this!*

Secondly, notice that those who planted seeds produced more LIFE and fruit. You need to understand that those who have a relationship with the King receive eternal Life, but the fruits that the trees yield are fruits for *today*. There is HOPE for today, MEANING for today and PEACE for today! Following the King gives one LIFE forever, but also LIFE for each day.

However, Kai'Ro, at times the fruit may be delayed. Those at the Garden received the fruit at different stages of their lives. Some immediately and others were well into their later years. But when the harvest was reaped, there was an abundance of fruit to share. Even with those who had none!

STORYTELLER: Sophia then grabbed Kai'Ro by the hand and led him gently out of the room and towards the exit.

SOPHIA: You have learned so much on this journey already.

KAI'RO: Back at Interpreter's house, I could hardly understand a thing until he explained it all to me.

SOPHIA: Wisdom is a divine gift from the King. You must pray for it, and He will give more to you. But you must also apply what knowledge you have gained to your life. Wisdom is putting Kingdom principles and knowledge to work in everyday life. The more you use it, the more you'll sidestep the pain and frustration that you can easily bring on yourself. Yet, it is also a blessing to those who watch your life. As you walk on the path of Wisdom, others will notice how your life is different from theirs. You will avoid many of the holes that others fall into due to their own foolishness and lack of understanding.

KAI'RO: I hear what you're sayin', but I don't know if anyone is really watchin' *my* life.

SOPHIA: (chuckling) Now, that's a foolish thing for you to say, Kai'Ro. Everyone you meet is watching your life. Some are observing much more closely than others. What about your brother, Lil' One?

KAI'RO: (hanging his head) Yeah. He was watchin' and look where it got him . . .

SOPHIA: But is it over for him? Do you think he is done watching and learning from you, his big brother? What about some of your old friends?

KAI'RO: I'm tryin' to get away from those bad memories and influences! I wouldn't mind gettin' out of the hood for good. You know, maybe get me a good job and a place to live in a nice neighborhood that doesn't have all the drama and nonsense.

SOPHIA: Kai'Ro, you must continue to see with an upside-down view. How many people have left the hood, left areas of decay and areas of pain simply to make their own life easier? Did not the King leave a place of peace and security for a place of danger and death? He left a platinum throne in Heaven and chose to be born in a wooden box full of animal spit and dirty straw. He gave up Streets of Gold to walk the dusty and stinking roads of this world. The King left a place where He ruled over angels and came to a place where mere men would show Him no respect, beat Him bloody and curse Him. Finally, they would kill Him.

KAI'RO: Yeah, you're right. I guess I just don't know if that's what I'm called to do.

SOPHIA: *Calling* is a curious thing. It's not *wrong* to live in the suburbs or in a community of peace, but hardly anyone ever claims that they're *called* to be in such a community. Why? Because to make such a decision is relatively easy. No one will second guess them. Yet, don't you think people should consider their calling no matter where they live? Just because a decision makes sense doesn't necessarily mean it's the right decision.

What I'm talking to you about right now, Kai'Ro, is not necessarily Wisdom; although Wisdom is part of such a decision. What I'm talking to you about now is Compassion. That is a choice to give up your LIFE and spend it on those who do not have life in them. It's the sacrificial step of following the King into a place where no one else would willingly go because they have fear, insecurity and doubt.

You can't get past sacrifice, Kai'Ro. Not if you really want to follow Him. Too many people cling to the comforts of this life instead. They are unwilling to give up the things that are dear to them—their material possessions. The desires of their eyes and greed for wealth become distractions that prevent them from following after the King. These folks give up their very soul in an attempt to gain this world around them. But can you put a price tag on your *soul*?

KAI'RO: I hear what you're sayin', but I'm also worried that my old crowd will drag me down again. There's too much temptation and bad memories back in the City of Doom!

SOPHIA: This is true. Yet, you have already come so far. You have grown in Wisdom. With the King's Word in your heart, and His Wisdom in your mind, He will guide you regarding whom you should help and from whom you should run. It is true that there are some old friends who would be better for you to run from. But there are also people there who need your help and need to see a life like yours to give them hope.

Remember this: there are always others whom the King has raised up to go on this journey with you. You don't have to go at it alone. You are *not* alone.

STORYTELLER: Kai'Ro stared hard at Sophia. He put both of his hands on his head and sighed.

KAI'RO: I will pray about what you're sayin' to me.

SOPHIA: (smiling) That is a good place to start. I am with you always, son.

STORYTELLER: There was a bright flash that caused Kai'Ro to cover his eyes. When he put his hands down again, Sophia and the CIRCUS OF WISDOM were gone. He was alone on the Heavenly Highway, and there were big decisions he had to make.

BROKEN AND THE HARVEST 16

STORYTELLER: Kai'Ro spun himself slowly in a circle looking at the road behind him and the road ahead. He had come so far, and now he didn't know exactly where to go.

KAI'RO: (to himself) What should I do? King, I cry out to You for direction. Fill my heart with Your heart and my mind with Your mind, so that I might better know what I've got to do.

STORYTELLER: As if in answer to his prayer, a young lady came walking down the road towards him. She was very thin and very pretty. Her head was bowed low and she was staring at the ground as she walked. Her arms were wrapped around her body as if she were trying to stay warm. As she drew closer, Kai'Ro could see that the girl was crying. Then, to his surprise, he recognized her!

KAI'RO: Broken? Is that you, girl?

STORYTELLER: Broken looked up, and when she saw Kai'Ro she smiled a little bit.

BROKEN: Kai'Ro? I can't believe it. I haven't seen you in the longest.

KAI'RO: Yeah. This is so crazy. What'cha doin'?

STORYTELLER: Broken looked back at the ground.

BROKEN: Nothin', for real. I'm just out walkin'.

KAI'RO: Didn't you graduate not too long ago?

BROKEN: (smiling) Top of the class.

KAI'RO: Girl, that's awesome. So you gotta be goin' to college, right? I mean, if anyone from our class could do it, it's you.

BROKEN: Yeah, see that's the thing. I ain't got no money to go to college.

KAI'RO: No money? Didn't you apply for scholarships? Top of the class and you didn't get no scholarships or nothin'?

BROKEN: I couldn't get my mama to fill out anything, Kai'Ro. (Crying again). She got back on the drugs again. And me and my lil' sister had to spend all kinds of time just tryin' to keep her from literally killin' herself. It was like all I could do just to care for her and then try to study to pass my tests. We had the power cut off at the house and even went for a long time with no food. Mama didn't reapply for food stamps. She was too strung out. Finally, a pastor got some folks from his church to straighten stuff out for us.

KAI'RO: But there was no way for you get some help with college?

BROKEN: Mama came to my graduation, ya know? She was all proud 'cause I was the first person to graduate from high school in my whole family's history. It was a big thing to me, and I was so proud of myself. I felt like I did somethin' honorable for my whole family. Well, about two days after graduation, I was tryin' to get my mama to fill out some financial paperwork for me. I think I would have qualified for the moon. My mama just put down the pen and pushed the paperwork away. Do you know what she said to me, Kai'Ro?

STORYTELLER: Broken burst into tears and had a really tough time pulling herself together.

BROKEN: She told me that the best thing I could do for myself and my future was to get pregnant and get on that Section 8. Can you believe that?

KAI'RO: What? Your mom told you to do that? That's craaazy! I'm so sorry she said that to you. I can't believe it. You didn't listen to that nonsense, did you?

BROKEN: I was crushed. I was mad. I ran outta the house and disappeared for like two weeks or somethin'. I guess I was just runnin' the streets. I had a friend 'round the way, a boy named No-Good, and so I hung out at his place.

STORYTELLER: Kai'Ro shook his head and then rubbed his hands down the sides of his face.

BROKEN: I couldn't believe my mama would say somethin' so ugly to me, particularly after me and my sister had done so much for her. Well, I finally went home and found out more bad news. The deadline for all those scholarships and financial aid had passed. I wouldn't get a dime. Plus, my mama was so strung out on drugs again that she couldn't hardly talk to me. Then, I found out the hardest news of all, Kai'Ro...

STORYTELLER: Kai'Ro looked at her and waited for her to speak.

BROKEN: (sniffing) I found out I was pregnant!

STORYTELLER: Broken fell forward and would have collapsed to the ground, but Kai'Ro leaned forward and caught her. He held her close while she bawled her eyes out on his chest. I could see tears rolling down his face as well, as he looked up to Heaven. Along the cracked Highway, he consoled Broken for a long time as she sobbed. Finally, Kai'Ro spoke.

KAI'RO: So, what'cha goin' to do now?

BROKEN: What'cha think? I'm goin' to be a mama now, and I'm goin' to get on that Section 8. My mama's words came true. Who knew I was goin' to do the exact thing she said?

KAI'RO: So, that's it? You're just tossin' all those college dreams in the trash, girl? You got no hope now?

BROKEN: What hope is there?

STORYTELLER: Broken wrestled free from Kai'Ro's hug and glared at him.

BROKEN: There ain't no hope for me, and there ain't no hope for the City of Doom neither. You know the place too. It's a death trap and nobody gets out...nobody goes anywhere. It's like a city for the dead. Don't talk about hope, like it's somethin' you can just go buy at the store and it can solve all ya problems. That ain't how it works, Kai'Ro!

STORYTELLER: Kai'Ro looked a bit shocked at her anger and seemed lost for words. Then I saw a fire emerge in his eyes, and he put a strong hand on her shoulder.

KAI'RO: You're right! Hope don't grow on trees. But hope ain't somethin' you can't find. Hope is real. And I've got hope. Look at me, girl! Right now I'm a high school dropout with no job and nowhere to live. I broke up with my girlfriend, Evangeline. My friends all left me when I needed them the most. And even before all that, I was just someone who fell into the cracks and into the dark spaces in the ground. I coulda stayed there, but I found hope. Yeah, I found it!

I'm not talkin' about no weak hope—the kind of weak hope you feel when you get a paycheck or make an "A" on a test. I'm talkin' 'bout a hope that's so deep and so real and so strong that I feel like I'm goin' to burst! I found that hope when I was the most hopeless. I was locked up like an animal for crimes I hadn't committed. Weighed down by my own guilt and shame, I just wanted to die. I'd been in and out of jail since I was a shortie and knew almost every cop in town by name. I'd done a lot of bad things...some that I'll never mention because they're too bad and too embarrassin' to talk about.

It was in that stinkin' jail, in a cell too small for a mouse—let alone a man—that I found hope. Through the bars of my cell, Preacher man came and talked to me. He introduced me to hope for the first time when he told me about a blameless and powerful King who was willin' to take all my shame and make it His shame. This perfect King was willin' to take all my guilt and make it His guilt. He was even willin' to take all my failures, shortcuts, goof-ups, screw-ups and every absurd thing I'd done—and accept blame for all of it—just for me.

That sounded good to me. I mean, I was a criminal, and this King was actually goin' to take my rap sheet and take the blame for it all. But then this guy told me somethin' that really shocked me. He told me that according to the Creator of the world, my rap sheet deserved the death penalty. In fact, he said that everyone has a rap sheet and everyone deserves the death penalty because that rap sheet offends a holy and perfect Creator.

But he said this blameless King was not goin' to let me die for those things. This King volunteered to die *Himself* for all those things. In fact, when He turned Himself in, they beat Him with their fists and with whips until nobody could recognize Him no more. Then, they stretched Him out on this big ol' Cross and pounded nine-inch spikes through His wrists and feet. All for me. The King hung up there for hours until He died. And He did this for me, and for you, Broken.

BROKEN: I don't know . . .

KAI'RO: Look, hopelessness is what sets in on ya when ya get to the point where all your struggles, failures, guilt and circumstances become like a stain on your soul that you can't get out no matter how hard you try. I mean, that's how I was in that jail. I wanted to die at that point 'cause I was weighed down by everything I'd done—all the lies I'd told, stuff I'd stole, all the people I'd hurt, and all the shame that went with those things. It was all a part of who I was. And, at that time, I felt like there was no way I'd ever be able to get rid of 'em or break free from 'em.

You're in that place now, Broken. Be honest with yourself, you made a mistake. In fact, you made a *bad* mistake, but that doesn't mean it's all over for ya now. It doesn't mean that all hope is lost. For those who love Him, the King that I follow promises that He'll work all things out for our good—even our shame and mistakes! Now, I don't know exactly how He's gonna do that for you. But I believe He will, if you're willin' to give your life and all that's in it to Him.

STORYTELLER: Broken stared at Kai'Ro. In her eyes, I could see a deep longing for Truth.

BROKEN: Word made it back to the City that you had gotten religious. A lot of people made fun of you and said it was just a matter of time before you came back to your old ways and your old friends. Fact is, I've had friends get religious on me before. And true enough, they ended up goin' back to their old ways and usually ended up goin' into stuff a lot worse. But you, you don't got no religion, Kai'Ro. It's like you gotta *relationship* with this King you've been talkin' about. You talk about Him as if He's your best friend or somethin'.

KAI'RO: He is.

BROKEN: I've never met nobody like you before. Back when you was in the City of Doom you were so strong, but you were angry and hard. You still look strong, but it's like, I don't know. It's like you have a whole new kinda strong. I can see it in your eyes. Thank you for talkin' with me, Kai'Ro. You've lifted me up.

KAI'RO: So, what'cha goin' to do now?

BROKEN: Well, I know what I'm *not* goin' to do.

KAI'RO: What's that?

BROKEN: I'm not goin' to give up. I'm not goin' on that Section 8 like Mama said I should.

KAI'RO: Yeah?

BROKEN: (smiling) Yeah!

KAI'RO: What about what I said 'bout the King?

BROKEN: Don't know yet. You gave me a lot to think about. I mean, everything you said hit me somewhere deep. I heard every word you said. I'm not sure I'm ready to give my life to no King just yet, but I'd sure like to have the same peace and strength I see in your face right now. If that's the only way to get it, well then, I might just give my life to Him.

KAI'RO: Sometimes that decision takes time. But when you give your life to the King, He gives you His Life in return. That's the biggest blessin'. Any peace, joy, hope, love or freedom you see in my life is 'cause He's livin' in me now. That's the biggest and best part about it. I'll pray for you, Broken. I'll pray that you find your life in His because you'll never be the same. I promise.

BROKEN: Thanks again, Kai'Ro. I hope to see you again. The City of Doom could use a man like you around. (Chuckling) That Armor you got on is goin' to cause a few people to crack, but I think it's cool. I think you'd do a whole lotta good.

STORYTELLER: The two hugged. Broken thanked him one more time and then turned back in the direction from which she had come. Kai'Ro watched her until she disappeared over the hill.

KAI'RO: (sighing and looking towards the sky) Okay, King, I think I'm gettin' the message. You want me to go back to my old stompin' grounds. I'll be honest, I don't feel like it at all. But You said in Your Word that the folks who bring Your Good News to the poor and to the lost have "beautiful feet." Someone with beautiful feet visited me in that jail cell a long time ago.

I'd be a thief and sellout if I didn't do the same for somebody else.

STORYTELLER: Kai'Ro paced back and forth for a while with his face pointed towards the heavens. His lips were moving, but in my dream I could not hear what he was saying.

Then he stopped and started walking back towards the city of his birth. He walked on for quite some time. His face was hard like flint, but in his eyes there was a softness and a love and a burning fire. The sun was high in the sky and beating down on him. Ahead was a tall shade tree. He walked over and leaned against it, enjoying the coolness it provided.

When he looked to his left, there was a crumbled brick wall. Graffitied on the side of the wall was the phrase, "The harvest is plentiful, but the workers are few." Kai'Ro smiled.

After resting for a period of time, he set off again until he came to a Crossroads. There was a sign leading to the City of Doom and another sign that went to a city called Tarshish.

KAI'RO: (to himself) Naw, I ain't goin' to be like Jonah and set off somewhere else...even though I don't feel like goin' back to the dreaded city I came from. The King told Jonah to go to a certain place. Part of him was afraid and part of him hated those people. So, he disobeyed the King and ended up in a fish's belly for like three days.

There's part of me that's afraid and, I'll be honest, there's a part of me that just don't wanna deal with a lot of those people back there in the City of Doom. But there ain't no way I want to end up in no belly of a fish. So I'm goin', O King! I'm goin'!

STORYTELLER: Kai'Ro walked and walked and walked. His mind was imagining all kinds of things. Sometimes his face got tense from fear. Other times, he smiled. After a great while, he made it back into the open countryside again. There were tall green trees, rolling hills and fresh air.

He stopped from time to time to soak it all up, breathing in the beauty. But before too long, he could see the dense smog off in the distance. There was a reddish black cloud just beyond the horizon. Kai'Ro squinted his eyes and could see the shadows of tall buildings hovering over the city. He exhaled a deep breath.

KAI'RO: (out loud) The City of Doom. A home for the lost and dyin'. A place where the streets are drenched with blood and the houses are full of horror. It's a city of killers, thieves and pimps. It's a place where women are nothin' more than property. Children are forgotten with the trash.

You may be the place where I was born, but you ain't my home no more. My home is in Heaven, and my Ruler is the King. Get ready. I'm comin' back to bring you Good News. I'm returnin' to give you some hope and point you towards Life.

That's right. Your ol' boy, Kai'Ro, is comin' back. But I ain't the same, and I pray you'll be ready. You may hear me or ya may hate me. Ya may hug me or ya may hit me. Ya might care for me or ya might kill me. But it don't matter, 'cause I'll love ya anyway. And I want to introduce you to the One Who can save ya. The King has sent me back...so here I come!

STORYTELLER: Suddenly, Kai'Ro took off in a sprint. He shot off down the old dirt road like lightning, kicking up a cloud of dust as he went. He stopped when he came to the old hedges just outside the city. He parted the bushes with his hands, crawled inside and disappeared from my sight.

Then, I awoke.

KAI'RO RETURNS

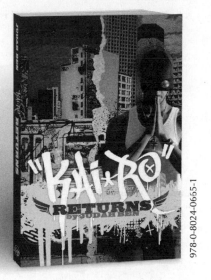

978-0-8024-0655-1

Kai'Ro Returns, follows the continued journey of Kai'Ro, an urban pilgrim. After finding the life and freedom he went searching for at the Cross, The King sends him back to the City of Doom as an ambassador of hope. He returns, haunted by past failures, an awareness of ruined relationships, and the damage he caused during his former life. He hopes that his transformed life and the power of the King can be used to rescue his community and friends from destruction.

"I'm personally excited about the work Judah Ben has done. To see his years of influence in the urban context fleshed out in writing is priceless. I'm honored to support him."
-Lecrae, Hip Hop recording artist

"The story of Kai'Ro shows the effects of how one man's choice to relocate to his old neighborhood with the hope of the Gospel makes a profound impact on changing his city for Christ."
-John Perkins, Founder of Christian Community Development Association

MOODY
PUBLISHERS
www.MoodyPublishers.com